"I think he *stabbed* me."

"All I saw was a brick. Are you sure?"

Loosening his grip, Noah looked down at his bicep. Blood was beginning to come through a slit in his jacket. "Yeah. I'm pretty sure he didn't do this with a brick."

Emily's stomach clenched as if she herself was injured. Yes, she was empathetic but this was more. Much more. Seeing Noah injured hit her right in the heart. "Why...?"

"Why what?" Noah asked, grimacing.

"Why did you get involved?"

His glance held accusation and when he said, "Why did you tell me to chase him?" Emily had no answer. All she could think of was being thankful that Noah had not been killed because of her. Losing innocent bystanders was always terrible. Losing a dear, dear friend would have been a tremendous personal loss.

A tragedy like that had nearly destroyed her once. She wasn't sure she could overcome it a second time.

Valerie Hansen was thirty when she awoke to the presence of the Lord in her life and turned to Jesus. She now lives in a renovated farmhouse on the breathtakingly beautiful Ozark Plateau of Arkansas and is privileged to share her personal faith by telling the stories of her heart for Love Inspired. Life doesn't get much better than that!

Books by Valerie Hansen

Love Inspired Suspense

Emergency Responders

Fatal Threat
Marked for Revenge
On the Run
Christmas Vendetta
Serial Threat

Rocky Mountain K-9 Unit

Ready to Protect

True Blue K-9 Unit: Brooklyn

Tracking a Kidnapper

True Blue K-9 Unit

Trail of Danger

Visit the Author Profile page at LoveInspired.com for more titles.

Serial Threat

Valerie Hansen

LOVE INSPIRED® SUSPENSE
INSPIRATIONAL ROMANCE

Recycling programs for this product may not exist in your area.

ISBN-13: 978-1-335-58728-2

Serial Threat

For questions and comments about the quality of this book, please contact us at CustomerService@Harlequin.com.

Love Inspired
22 Adelaide St. West, 41st Floor
Toronto, Ontario M5H 4E3, Canada
www.LoveInspired.com

Printed in U.S.A.

My times are in thy hand:
deliver me from the hand of mine enemies,
and from them that persecute me.
—*Psalm* 31:15

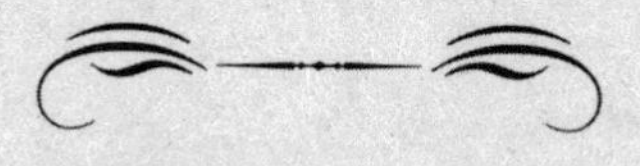

To new friends and old friends and those I have yet to meet.
Every one of you is a special blessing.

ONE

The Paradise, Missouri, patrol car rolled to a stop beneath an overhead light in the deserted parking lot. "Unit three on scene, City Park," Emily Zwalt radioed as she swept the mounted spotlight over the short-cropped grass and past picnic tables. "No sign of the disturbance that was reported." She cautiously stepped out of the car. "No female screaming. I don't hear anything."

"Copy. Your discretion," the dispatcher replied.

Emily stood to don her uniform jacket and hat, then spoke to her partner. "I'll do a sweep down by the lake, Cal. You take the high ground. Okay?"

"Whatever. You don't have blond hair or blue eyes, so you're probably not on the serial killer's hit list."

"Not funny. Especially to the victims. Show some compassion, will you?"

"Yeah, yeah, I'll try." He adjusted his belt. "Radio me when you're ready to give up this wild goose chase."

"Speaking of geese," Emily said in parting, "watch your step around the ones that live here. They bite."

"Same to you. You'll be closer to the water than I will."

Leaving him, she played the powerful beam of her

flashlight over the terrain. Low fog blanketed the man-made lake and partially obscured her path. Shivering, she turned up the collar of her jacket. Maybe it was the fog, maybe the predicted storm, but the park felt unusually creepy tonight, as if the air was charged with malevolence.

A rustling noise and movement in Emily's peripheral vision startled her. She whirled. A small flock of Canada geese that had bedded down on the lakeshore was stirring.

"It's okay, guys," Emily murmured, hoping to soothe the half-wild birds with a human voice. "I'm a friend."

A dry branch cracked. She froze. Most of the wary birds were staring into the dimness to her left. Contours of the land and the large body of water might be distorting sound as she interpreted it, but nothing fooled geese.

"Help!" echoed faintly.

There it is! Emily dropped into a crouch, her hand on the grip of her holstered weapon. The geese scattered and began to go berserk, honking and flapping their wings, their necks stretched long, heads held high.

A large, dark form was starting to appear in the fog. Tensing, she drew her gun and announced, "Paradise police."

As she began to straighten, a masked figure caught her off-balance. She tried to dodge, but his shoulder hit her hard and sent her reeling. Rolling on the ground to bring her .38 to bear on the assailant, she shouted, "Freeze! Police!"

The black-clad figure had passed, and she thought he would keep going. Instead, he turned and came at her again!

There was no time to get to her feet, no chance to

face her foe on an equal plane, so she double-gripped the .38 and steadied her aim. “Stop!”

A slight pause was accompanied by a deep, menacing laugh. Whoever this was, he wasn’t afraid of her or the gun, acting as though he was sure she wouldn’t shoot. “I said, freeze.”

The geese were making an awful racket nearby. Emily backpedaled, kept her eyes on her attacker and managed to key her radio. “Officer needs assistance.”

“Copy. Where are you?”

Just as she started to reply, she saw the man’s gaze shift to a place over her shoulder and focus there. He wasn’t alone!

Piercing pain wrapped her head in a band of agony.

Needles of colored lights pierced her vision.

Blackness crept in at the edges of her mind until the last vestiges of her initial attacker vanished and she collapsed into the pure darkness of unconsciousness.

Newly returned to Paradise, attorney Noah Holden had spent a quiet evening at home, going over briefs for upcoming court actions, and had nodded off at his desk. When his cell phone roused him, it took only a second for his senses to catch up.

“Holden.”

“It’s me.” The voice was quavering and high.

“Who is this?”

“Me. Buddy Corrigan.”

Noah sighed. Of course. Would he never learn that giving out his private number was a bad idea? “Why are you calling me at—” he checked the time “—three in the morning?”

“Sorry. But I just remembered something important.”

Noah reached for a pen and paper. “Okay. Go ahead.”

"Not over the phone. Face-to-face."

"Then call my office and make an appointment."

"That might be too late. If you don't come tonight, they may get to me before I can tell you."

Another sigh. Noah shook his head, knowing he was going to cave and hoping the client was telling the truth. "Okay. Where and when?"

"Now. I'll be at the gazebo in the park. You know where that is?"

"Unless they've moved it. I haven't been back in town long enough to take notice." Pausing, he waited for a reply before realizing the caller had broken the connection. At this point he really had no choice unless he intended to leave his client to the possible lethal actions of whoever he was afraid of.

Donning a leather bomber jacket, Noah headed for the clandestine meeting. Of course he had misgivings. Who wouldn't? But at least this was tiny, peaceful Paradise instead of Kansas City or St. Louis, where he'd practiced law in the past. Up there, he'd had a permit to carry a concealed weapon but, because being armed hadn't seemed necessary here, he'd locked away his firearm. As he drove along the deserted streets toward the outskirts of town, however, he began to wonder if venturing out unarmed had been wise.

Approaching the park from the north, he saw a pulsating blue-and-red glow far across the lake. If the gazebo had been over there, he would have immediately assumed he was too late.

Parking, Noah checked his phone. There had been no texts or voice mail messages since the call that had awakened him, so he climbed out of the car.

"Buddy? I'm here," he announced in a normal voice as he approached the gazebo. A fresh coat of white paint made it stand out even at night, and the light built into his cell phone helped him see the ground.

"Buddy?"

Still no reply. Hair prickled at the nape of Noah's neck. He figured he could stay at the gazebo where he'd be easy to see or fall back and watch from a position of relative safety. Prudence insisted he step aside.

Circling the leading edge of the lattice-covered structure, he found a copse of azaleas leafed out and ready to bloom. The bushes offered perfect camouflage. He sidled closer and waited. Buddy Corrigan was likely to pop up any second, providing the police across the lake hadn't scared him off, and he'd be ready.

As Noah pushed his shoulder in among the tender new branches, the side of his foot bumped into a rock, or so he thought until he tried to step past it and realized it was quite large.

One arm pushed aside the leaves so he could shine his light on the ground. He froze.

"Buddy?" Seeing the prone body had made him think it was that of his client until his brain began to function better. This was a woman. He quickly crouched to check for a pulse and found none, but she was still warm. Maybe it wasn't too late.

Grabbing her shoulder, he rolled her onto her back. Lifeless eyes stared at him. She was clearly beyond CPR.

Noah straightened, lifted his cell phone and called 911. "I want to report a murder."

"Nonsense. I'm fine," Emily insisted. "I'm not going to the hospital for a little bump on the head."

Her chief wasn't convinced. He nodded to her partner. "Dodge, you take Officer Zwalt, circle around, and bring your unit in from the north." He paused with a scowl. "And keep an eye on her. If she so much as looks at you funny, haul her back here. I'll have an ambulance standing by."

"Yes, sir." Cal's smug expression made Emily grit her teeth. The problem was, in this instance, Chief Rowlings was right. A possibly injured officer like herself needed to be watched, even sidelined, until proven capable.

The short drive around the park perimeter was nearly over when a new dispatch sent Emily's pulse into overdrive. "Reported body found, north end of the park. All available units respond."

Cal flipped the switch for the light bar and hit the siren, and they careened into a parking lot seconds later.

"Unit three on scene, north lot," Emily radioed. "One vehicle, Missouri license plate." She recited the numbers and letters. "No driver or passengers visible."

Cal was ahead of her, gun drawn, moving cautiously toward a gazebo. She heard him yell, "Freeze! Police! Hands up."

Capture that quickly was rare, but she followed his lead and drew her sidearm, keeping it pointed away from her partner.

"Light him up," Cal ordered.

Emily aimed her powerful flashlight at the face of the dark-haired suspect. His hands were raised, his eyes squinting against the bright beam, and she was so astonished her jaw dropped. "Noah?"

"On your knees," Cal shouted. "Hands behind your back."

Standard procedure would have led Emily to secure the suspect. Instead, she countered with, "Stand down, Cal. I know him."

Cal's head snapped around, his aim never wavering. "I don't care if he's your long-lost brother. Cuff him."

"Hey! I just reported the body, that's all. I have nothing to do with all this," Noah insisted.

Because he had not knelt on command, Emily stepped directly in front of him. No one had informed her that Noah was back in town, and encountering him there, like that, was a shock. However, the last thing she wanted was to see her old friend in danger from a gung ho rookie like her partner.

Emily whirled with her back to Noah and faced Cal, hands partially raised as a caution. "I said, stand down. We owe this man the right to explain."

Her partner lowered his gun as he radioed but didn't holster it. "Unit three. Suspect in custody."

From behind her came the almost forgotten voice. "Thanks."

She spoke over her shoulder. "You're welcome. You reported a crime?"

"Yes. There's a body on the other side of the gazebo."

"Did you recognize the victim?"

Noah's "no" didn't surprise her since he hadn't been in Paradise for—she mentally calculated—at least ten years.

A stern glance at Cal's weapon and a tilt of her head was enough to convince him to holster the gun, but she could tell he was anything but convinced. Fortunately, the sounds of approaching sirens seemed to placate him.

"Okay, show me." Emily turned and played her light over the gazebo and surrounding terrain, following Noah's directions.

"There. Under those bushes. See her?"

"Yes." She made her way closer, Noah at her side.

Experience told the sad story, yet she bent to make sure and found no pulse.

Blood pounded and Emily's head wound throbbed as she straightened. This victim was a match for three others who had been murdered recently and dropped in her little town. The serial killer had struck again, and they were looking at the actual scene of the crime. This time, Lord willing, they might have a chance of finding clues to who was taking innocent lives.

"I have one confirmed victim," Emily radioed. "No suspect, just the reporting party. Requesting crime scene techs. Cancel the ambulance."

Cops were fanning out on foot to search the rest of the park while Emily guarded the crime scene. "Tell me you didn't touch her."

"I had to roll her over to see if she was alive. You didn't expect me to just leave her lying there if I could help, did you?"

"It would have been sensible to wait for the police."

Noah was shaking his head. "No way. I had to be sure she was dead."

"I suggest you choose a different way to phrase that when you're questioned officially," Emily warned. "That sounds an awful lot like a confession."

TWO

Officer Calvin Dodge was the object of Chief Rowlings's ire when he arrived. "You should have asked for ID and checked with dispatch."

"He was found with the body, sir."

"Because he tripped over it and made the 911 call."

It was all Emily could do to hide her grin. Cal had a tendency to jump to conclusions, and she was pretty sure they had been paired because of her cautious stability. Trouble was, Cal usually failed to heed her sensible suggestions.

Ignoring Emily, Noah approached the chief and extended his right hand.

"Good to see you again," Rowlings said, shaking hands. "How's Max?"

"Recovering. Some strokes are worse than others. I'm just glad I was available to come help with his law practice."

"I'm sure Max is, too," said the older man. "So, what happened here?"

Noah began to fill him in while Emily listened. "At 3:00 a.m. I got a call from a new client, Buddy Corrigan. He said somebody was after him, and he wanted to meet in secret. That's what brought me to the park in the middle of the night. Only she—" Noah gestured toward the victim "—was the only person I saw when I got here."

Rowlings had been nodding. When he stopped, Emily wondered what he was thinking. She had plenty of questions she wanted to ask Noah, most of which had nothing to do with crime.

She noted her chief's relaxed body language and wondered if Noah realized how well rehearsed it was. Rowlings's good-old-boy persona was perfect for a small town. It could also disappear in a flash when he was speaking with the press or other high-ranking lawmen.

"So," the chief drawled, "how'd you manage to find her tucked away like she is? I mean, if I didn't know where she was, I wouldn't have noticed her, 'specially not in the dark."

"I was hiding back there," Noah said, mirroring Rowlings's posture and stuffing his hands in his pockets. "I figured if somebody was after Buddy, they might mistake me for him and take a potshot."

Emily was relieved to hear her chief say, "Smart. Course that's to be expected, you bein' a college boy and all."

Noah smiled for the first time since her arrival, and the sight sent a tingle up her spine that had nothing to do with chilly temperatures. "College can only teach so much. Common sense is necessary too."

"Can't argue with that, son," Rowlings said, once again subtly indicating his superior position by lowering Noah's. Emily had seen this technique work before, and close observation of Noah told her that he had, too, because although his mouth continued to smile, that emotion never reached his dark eyes.

When Rowlings looked to her and said, "You do the debriefing and write me a full report, Zwalt," Emily had to stop herself from reacting. This was not the time to appear anything but professional, particularly concerning Noah Holden, yet inside she was both elated and nervous. Outside, where all could see, she was as cool as a glass of sweet tea on a summer's day.

Facing Noah, she swept an arm toward the parking area. "My car's back there. Shall we?"

"As long as you promise to let me out when we're done." This time, his lopsided smile brought a familiar twinkle to his eyes and made her stomach lurch. This was the Noah she had known ten years ago, the man who used to make her teenage heart race with a glance, yet who had remained oblivious to her blossoming devotion. He'd broken her heart by leaving town without a goodbye and had stayed away until now. Whatever tenuous connection they may once have had, it had vanished long ago.

Emily led the way to the car and opened the passenger side for him. "Please."

Shrugging, he slid in, leaving one foot on the pavement so she couldn't slam the door.

"Don't be afraid, Mr. Holden. You're not under arrest."

"Never was," he said nonchalantly. "You didn't read me my rights."

Emily circled to the driver's side and positioned herself behind the wheel. If Noah had been anyone else, she would have questioned him outside the vehicle where she'd have had full access to her weapon, but this was different. He was different. And, truth to tell, so was she.

"Name, address and phone number?" she asked, ready to type it into the car's computer station.

He rattled off that information, then went on. “Age thirty-two, attorney at Max Maxwell and Associates for the time being, happily unmarried and no pets. You?”

“I’m the one asking the questions, Mr. Holden.”

“There you go with the Mr. again. Why?”

“Because I’m an officer of the law, and you’re a suspect.”

“Your chief seemed to think otherwise. Do you disagree?”

“The Noah Holden I used to know wouldn’t hurt anyone,” she said. “I was afraid Cal might shoot you when you refused to cooperate with him.” She waved her hands as if erasing an invisible whiteboard. “Forget I said that.”

Noah was chuckling. “Not in a million years. I always did love your candor. Glad to see that hasn’t changed. And thanks for stepping between me and the gun, by the way.”

“You noticed.”

“Uh-huh. That’s a side of you that’s new to me. How long have you been a police officer?”

“Two years.”

By keeping her eyes on the computer screen, Emily was able to control her expression. At least, she hoped she was. Rationalizing helped. After all, this was an acquaintance from her past. It was normal to be glad to see him again. “For the record, tell me everything, starting with your reason for being in town.”

“You heard your chief. I came back when Maxwell’s office assistant contacted me about his stroke. He had invited me to join his practice in the past, and I’d always put him off. This time I had no choice. I had to come.”

“So your presence in Paradise is temporary?”

“I sure hope so.”

Emily noticed that his focus had changed, and he was gazing out the windshield at the crime scene tape being strung from tree to tree, so she asked, "Tell me about this client who's supposed to have called you tonight."

She'd phrased her query that way to goad him. He didn't take the bait. "Buddy Corrigan. Barely out of his teens. He was arrested for drunk driving and vandalism. I'm representing him pro bono on Max's orders."

"How did he get your private number? I assume that's how he reached you at home in the middle of the night."

"Yeah. My mistake. I don't usually share personal information, but he looked like such a good kid, I let down my guard."

"I learned a long time ago to avoid doing that. It's tough enough staying anonymous in a small town."

"Tough? It's impossible. Why do you think I joined a practice in St. Louis? I hate small towns."

Emily finally let herself smile. "Too bad. I love it here. Wouldn't want to live anywhere else."

"Whatever floats your boat," Noah quipped, starting to lean toward the open door. "Are we done?"

"I think so." Saving the file, Emily got out. "We'll know where to find you if we have more questions."

Walking around to his side of the patrol car, she offered to shake his hand. Hers was extended toward him when the sound of a gunshot echoed across the rolling hills. A side window of the cruiser shattered.

Emily yelled, "Get down!"

When Noah didn't duck fast enough, she took him to the ground with a body slam that knocked the wind out of both of them.

"I said, get *down*."

Coughing and gasping, he stared up at her. "Was that a gunshot?"

"Yes." This wasn't the right time to lecture him, so she held her tongue while she levered herself to her knees. "Are you going to be sensible and stay down there, or do I have to cuff you after all?"

Hands held above his head as if in surrender, Noah said, "I'm good. Go get 'em, Officer."

Emily didn't waste time being offended, nor did she laugh. It was troubling to hear Noah joking about being shot at, but she had bigger problems right now. They all did.

Noah felt a pang of concern as he watched Emily draw her gun and join the charge toward the supposed origin of the gunshot. What a crazy profession. Sensible folks ran the other way when they were being shot at. He certainly would have if he hadn't been so shocked. Had to give Em credit for her reaction time, though. Boy, was she fast. And effective, he thought, rubbing the back of his head where it had slammed into the asphalt and brushing tiny chunks of safety glass off his jacket.

Raised on one elbow, he looked around. Court cases had taught him the protocol of a murder investigation. A uniformed officer had remained with the body, as had somebody with a camera who was taking crime scene photos prior to the arrival of forensic technicians. Other than that, being basically alone, he decided to take shelter in the police car.

A shotgun was clamped upright between the front seats. Noah would have picked it up if it hadn't been locked in place. Nearly every kid who grew up in Paradise knew how to shoot and handle guns safely, including him, and for the second time that night, he wished he was armed.

His thoughts drifted to the victim he'd stumbled over. She was young. And pretty. And very, very dead. If he believed for a second that Buddy had called to set him up for the murder, he'd drop the guy like the business end of Taser wires, Max or no Max. The thing was, he couldn't see that dumb kid coming up with something so devious.

Since Noah was hunkered down in the seat, he failed to notice anyone's approach until a gun barrel appeared in his peripheral vision and a gruff male voice ordered him to raise his hands. "Hey, I'm just an innocent bystander," he said. "I ducked in here when the shooting started."

"You're not a cop?"

"No way." Quelling the urge to announce his profession, he fell silent instead. If he turned his head slightly, he could probably see the mirror image of whoever was holding the gun on him. If this man wasn't with the police department, however, his face might be the last one Noah ever saw. He wasn't willing to take that chance.

Seconds became minutes. Beads of sweat dotted his forehead, and one trickled into his right eye. The longer he sat there with his hands raised, the more he was sure he wasn't being confronted by a police officer.

Finally, he'd taken all the stress his nerves would stand. "Can I put my hands down now?"

There was no answer. Noah chanced a sidelong glance, then turned his head. No gun, no gunman, no more threat. "Whew."

His ragged breathing had not yet returned to normal when Emily returned. She was gesturing and speaking loudly before she reached him. “All clear. Chief says you can go. We know where to find you.”

Noah got out, remaining close to the open car door. “Not until you dust this window frame and the metal around it for prints. Somebody just threatened me with a gun, and he may have left clues on the car.”

“Not funny.” Emily made a face of disgust.

It hadn’t occurred to him that she might doubt his story. He grabbed her wrist when she reached toward the door handle. “Don’t touch that. I’m not kidding.”

The way she was looking at his grip told him it was putting her off. Well, tough. This was serious. Deadly serious.

“I’m not playing games with you, Em.” Noah made eye contact without a flinch. “Somebody, a man, held a gun to my head while you were gone. When he found out I wasn’t a cop, he disappeared.”

“Disappeared? Like, poof?”

“No. Like I wasn’t worth wasting a bullet on.”

“What did he look like?”

“I never saw him. I was turned away when he showed up. All I could see was what looked like the edge of a finger resting on the window frame.”

“Where, exactly?”

Noah pointed.

“Okay.” She radioed her chief and was told to protect the possible prints until a member of the evidence team got to her.

Finally, she asked the question Noah had been waiting for. “Are you all right, Mr. Holden?”

“No.”

“No?” The pitch of her voice rose. “You’re injured?”

“Yes. My pride has taken a terrible beating. Worse

than being shot at and blamed for murder, an old friend is refusing to speak my name."

"Your friend is probably concerned about proper protocol."

That was almost enough to make him laugh despite the scare he'd had. He did allow himself a slight smile. "Hmm, maybe she's forgotten where we are. This is Paradise, Missouri, just slightly bigger than your average mud puddle with a population you could jam into four or five school buses, if you had to."

There was no corresponding smile on Emily's face when she said, "It's also the town where somebody has been dumping the bodies of female victims, all in their early twenties, all with blond hair and blue eyes, just like the one you found."

Noah could see how empathetic she was and rued his joke. "I'm sorry. I had no idea. You should have told me."

"You had no need to know."

"So why tell me now?"

Sadness in her expression touched him deeply and made him want to reach out to her, to comfort her with a supportive embrace. He was wise enough to squelch the impulse.

"I told you because I think you're in this mess up to your eyeballs, *Noah*, whether you realize it or not."

There was no way he was going to argue with her, because he agreed. How or why was still unanswered, but like it or not, she was dead right.

THREE

"Chief Rowlings will probably want to speak to you himself," Emily told Noah.

"How long has this Paradise crime wave been going on? I haven't heard anything about it."

"Very few people outside law enforcement have. We're trying to keep a lid on it for as long as possible."

Emily noticed he was striking the same nonchalant pose he'd used in dealing with the chief and guessed it was standard, especially in potentially touchy situations. When he said, "Is that fair to vulnerable young women?", she was sure he cared more than his body language indicated.

"Chief Rowlings makes important decisions like that," Emily said. "It's above my pay grade."

"I imagine that's a relief."

"It is." Idle chatting seemed inappropriate for their situation, yet Emily hated to end it. "We'll need all the information you have on Buddy Corrigan."

"Most of what I know came from police files and court proceedings."

"Just the same, I know the chief will want to see any notes you may have made and hear any conversations you recorded."

Noah chuckled wryly. "You know I can't share that. Client privilege prohibits it."

"I figured it was worth a try, considering. You were shot at, and a gun was held to your head."

"And both times I was in or near a police car."

"True." She had to give him points for discernment. "But don't forget how you ended up here at the park."

"I'm not likely to." Noah pushed back his cuff to check his watch. "It's probably too early to roust Buddy, but I intend to get to the bottom of this. He'd better have a good excuse."

"Do you really think he's involved?"

"I can't imagine how or why," Noah said.

Emily had come to the same conclusion. Nothing about the small-time lawbreaker pointed to a violent nature. "Did you recognize his voice on the phone?"

"Can't say I did. The caller sounded scared, though."

"That's pretty weak proof. Whoever it was may have been forced into it."

Judging by the rising arch of Noah's brows and tilt of his head, he hadn't considered that possibility and was far from accepting the concept. "Why? I haven't been back in town long enough to ruffle feathers, let alone make somebody mad enough to want to frame me."

"You're sure about that?"

"Positive."

"And you haven't given Buddy any reason to do this to you?"

"Of course not. I got him out on bail."

Emily sighed, folded her arms across her chest and stared at him solemnly. "You do realize that the only thing left is to consider that you may be guilty, right?"

* * *

Trusting the letter of the law to bring fairness only went so far with Noah. His studies had provided enough cases of perverted justice to leave him concerned, and so far he'd been unable to wipe Emily's comment from his thoughts. Was that why she'd made it? Was she trying to get him to help her solve the crime, or did she actually believe he could commit murder? The former was ridiculous, and the latter was not acceptable, either.

A brief internet search gave him her home address but no phone number. That wasn't unusual since most folks these days used cell phones, so what he decided to do was pick up Buddy, question him about the call, then take him over to Emily's. It didn't matter whether the guy admitted or denied it. At least Noah would have living proof. That should allay suspicion until his phone provider was able to come up with a list of his call activity. Then all he'd have to do is prove he hadn't attacked and killed the victim after he got to the park.

He located Corrigan having breakfast in a local diner just off the Paradise town square and joined him in a back booth. "Hey, Buddy. How's it going?"

"Great. I didn't get fired 'cause you got me sprung, and I only missed a day's work."

"Good." Noah signaled the waitress by turning over the clean cup waiting on the table and lifting it in her direction. As soon as he had his coffee, he refocused on Buddy. "So, why did you call me last night?"

"Huh?" The younger man stopped shoveling scrambled eggs into his mouth.

"Last night. About 3:00 a.m."

"I didn't call nobody last night."

Noah sipped his hot coffee and observed his client.

Either this guy was the best liar he'd ever met or he truly had no idea what was going on.

"You hear about the murder?"

That sent Buddy leaning back as far as the booth would allow. "What are you talking about?"

"You didn't ask me to meet you in the park last night?"

Buddy raised both hands. "No way. Honest. All I've been doing since the judge cut me loose is mindin' my own business."

"Okay." Noah nodded and drank more coffee, biding his time. "What hours do you work today?"

"Two to nine. Why?"

"Because when you finish here, you and I are going to take a little ride."

Wariness painted Buddy's face, and Noah noted his clenching fists. "I don't think so."

"I do." Noah picked up the bill lying on the table and stood to pull out his wallet. "Finish your breakfast. I'll leave the tip and take care of this for you. Meet me outside."

If he had had the slightest inkling that his client would duck out the back door instead of joining him, he would have stayed, drinking coffee, for as long as it took. Unfortunately, by the time he'd finished at the cash register and turned around, Buddy's table was already empty. Adding insult to his good deed, the bills he'd left for the tip were missing, too.

More than a little disgruntled, Noah replaced his tip and straight-armed the swinging half doors leading to the kitchen. Two cooks were tending a grill. "Did you see Buddy Corrigan run through here?"

All he got was a couple of noncommittal shrugs, so

he kept going and checked the alley. Other than smelly trash, the area was deserted. So was the side street.

Ideas were jelling as Noah climbed into his car. He'd make a couple of passes through town, just in case he could spot Buddy, then head for Emily's house. Yes, his excuse for visiting had disappeared, but that didn't mean he couldn't go talk to her. Maybe, if he made friendly overtures, she'd be less likely to suspect him of committing a crime.

Disgusted by that train of thought, Noah grimaced. He'd never been a manipulative person in his private life even though doing so was necessary to convince prosecutors and juries. Had learning to do that changed his outlook on life in general?

For a brief moment, his sentiments came into question. He banished doubt by reminding himself he was doing the job to which he had dedicated himself—helping the downtrodden and innocent. That was his calling, the special gift he had vowed to use for good when he'd been deeply moved by the evident need.

"And speaking of innocent men," Noah muttered, "look at me."

An early morning jog had been part of Emily's daily routine for years. Despite being on duty some nights, she rarely skipped her run, although this morning she did cut it short.

Wiping her brow and draping a small towel around her neck, she grabbed a cup of coffee and a granola bar, carrying them to her porch swing.

Traffic in the quiet street was sparse enough that she saw only two cars pass while she ate and relaxed. Thoughts of Noah Holden had crowded her mind the night before and were still refusing to go away, so she was happy for the diversion when one of the neighborhood cats jumped onto the swing beside her. "Well, good morning to you, Missy. Catch any mice lately?"

The tabby rubbed against her side and meowed.

"Sorry. You missed breakfast. I need a coffee refill, so I'll go see what I can find for you, too. Don't go away."

Her visitor was pacing at the screen door when she returned. "Here you go, kitty. Leftover chicken."

Not wanting to accidentally pour scalding hot coffee on the friendly cat, she set her mug on the porch railing before crouching to share the tidbit.

The cat had been purring loudly. Suddenly, it stiffened and hissed, its back arching and the hair on its tail standing out like a bottlebrush.

Startled, Emily wondered if she'd done something to scare the poor, hungry cat. An instant later she knew otherwise, because she sensed danger, too. A shadow fell across the porch. The cat bolted, almost knocking Emily over.

She regained her balance and straightened, reaching for the mug of steaming coffee, then drawing back her arm as she started to turn.

Someone was there, all right. A large person dressed all in black had a brick in one hand and appeared ready to strike.

She'd shed her shoes, phone, water bottle and concealed carry pistol when she'd arrived home, so she was basically unarmed—except for the coffee.

That flew directly at the attacker, splashing against his ski mask and flooding the eye holes.

He yelped, dropped the brick and turned tail.

Just as he vaulted over the railing at the end of the porch, a silver BMW was pulling into her driveway.

Emily didn't wait. She shouted, "Get him!" pointed to the far end of the porch and raced back inside for her gun. A few seconds later she realized who had been in the car and wondered if Noah would be of any help or if he'd just sit there because he didn't know what was going on.

She yanked open the kitchen door, hoping to cut off the man, her gun at the ready. The small backyard was empty.

Off the porch in one leap, she landed on rocky ground and wished she hadn't shed her shoes. The yard looked empty, and there was only one other place her attacker could have gone so quickly. The neighbor's yard.

A board fence separated their two city lots. Emily knew better than to peer over the top and expose herself to danger, so she approached cautiously. Listening. Moving closer and closer.

As she reached the corner of her house, she was ready for anything, or so she thought. She whipped around the corner in a shooter's stance and came face-to-face with Noah!

The gun muzzle instinctively pointed skyward. "Did you see him?"

Noah nodded, and it was then that Emily noticed his strange expression. She was about to demand *Which way did he go?* when she realized Noah was gripping his upper arm.

"I don't know. It all happened so fast." He leaned the opposite shoulder against the house and stared at her before he added, "I think he *stabbed* me."

"All I saw was a brick. Are you sure?"

Loosening his grip he looked down at his bicep. Blood was beginning to ooze through a slit in his jacket. "Yeah. I'm pretty sure he didn't do this with a brick."

Her stomach clenched as if she herself was injured. Yes, she was empathetic, but this was more. Much more. Seeing Noah actually hurt hit her right in the heart. She reached for him without thinking and touched the back of the hand he was using to staunch the blood, as if she could somehow render aid that way. "Why…?"

"Why what?" Noah asked, grimacing.

"Why did you get involved?"

His glance held accusation, and when he said, "Why did you tell me to chase him?" Emily had no answer. All she could think of was being thankful that Noah had not been killed because of her. Losing innocent bystanders was always terrible. Losing a dear, dear friend would have been a tremendous personal loss.

A tragedy like that had nearly destroyed her once. She wasn't sure she could handle it a second time.

FOUR

The last thing Noah wanted to do was admit how foolish he felt, regardless of her spontaneous request for help. Unfortunately, the gash in his arm spoiled any attempt at nonchalance. It hurt. And the bleeding concerned him enough to consider medical treatment. What he had not expected was Emily's reaction. He hadn't wanted her to fuss over him, but seeing her turn her back on him to stand like a human shield for the second time in two days was surprisingly off-putting.

"He's long gone," Noah insisted. "You can relax."

"As soon as backup arrives, I will," she said, holding out one hand. "Give me your phone. Mine's in the house."

He handed it over and listened while she reported the attack and requested assistance. "And send an ambulance. I have one victim on scene."

"I don't need an ambulance," Noah argued. "It's just a scratch."

"Standard procedure," Emily said. "Can you walk?"

"He stabbed my arm, not my leg."

"Yeah, well, you're a little pale. Not going to pass out on me, are you?"

"I've never fainted in my life." Noah realized that they were snapping at each other but didn't try to soften his replies. The more angry he was, the more adrenaline would flow, and the easier it would be for him to tolerate pain—or whatever happened next.

Emily huffed. "There's a first time for everything. Work your way along the side of the house to the back door while I cover you. Let's move."

Although it would have been satisfying to argue with her, Noah could see the good sense of obeying. This time. By keeping his uninjured shoulder against the side of the house in case he did need the support, he made good time to the corner. That's when she put out a hand to stop him.

"I go first."

"Are you sure all this drama is necessary, Officer Zwalt?" Noah couldn't help taunting her despite his injury. There was just something *off* about letting her shepherd him along. He should be protecting her, not the other way around.

Disgusted, he waited for her to give the all clear. He might be bigger and stronger, but he was also leaving a trail of red drops and, like it or not, his chance to play the hero had ended when he'd become a victim.

Emily's hand appeared from the blind corner, groping. Still keeping pressure on his wound, Noah reached out with his free hand, then moaned when she tugged, because that was his injured side.

There was concern in her expression as she glanced back. "Sorry. Keep up, okay?"

"Gotcha."

The porch steps lay ahead. Emily hesitated, so he mirrored her action before asking, "Why are we stopping?"

"I left the door unlocked. We don't know if the assailant actually ran away or doubled back and entered the house."

"I watched him running off."

She was nodding. "That's assuming he was alone."

"I didn't see anybody else."

"Good."

Noah could tell by her body language that she had made a decision. His back was against the house as they sidled up the stairs together. He thought she might go inside first to clear the house, but she opened the door with a hard push and sent him ahead while she closed and locked it behind them.

Before he had a chance to question that decision, Emily provided the answer. "I figured there was more danger leaving you exposed outside than there would be bringing you in. It was a calculated risk."

"Understood. Thanks."

"Just doing my job," she answered flatly. "Stay away from the windows while I check the rest of the house."

She had her gun in one hand, cell phone in the other, and was making a call as she left him. "The victim is ambulatory. I have him in the house with me. Injuries don't appear life-threatening unless an artery was nicked."

Noah had already thought of that. Since there was no discernible pulse coming from his injury he figured he'd be okay. He was, however, making a mess in Emily's kitchen, so he grabbed a towel off the sink and pressed it to his arm to slow the bleeding, then took a seat at the small table in the corner.

He had just gotten settled when Emily returned. It was a relief to see her pistol holstered. "All clear?"

She nodded. "Yes. How are you doing?"

"I've been better," he replied, starting to smile and wondering why it felt so good to have her close by again. "What happened, anyway? When I drove up, all you said was, 'Get him.'"

"I am sorry about that." She joined him at the table. "I should never have involved you. It was a reflex action, and I regret it."

"Yeah, me, too," Noah said, letting his smile grow and arching an eyebrow. "This smarts."

"Undoubtedly."

"Sorry about the mess. I'd have cleaned it up if I hadn't had to keep pressure on my arm."

Emily shrugged. "It's nothing. I'm used to it."

"You have people bleeding all over your kitchen on a regular basis?" He purposely mimicked astonishment and was rewarded by her soft laugh.

"No. I meant injuries. I do my share of stabilizing wounds on the job while we wait for an ambulance."

Sobering, Noah leaned back in his chair and sighed. "Do you often get attacked?"

"No. Not often. And I usually have plenty of backup on scene."

"Armed, you mean. I get it. I have a concealed carry permit, but I put my gun away when I came back to Paradise. Now I wonder if I still need it."

The sobering look Emily gave him told him as much as her words. "Until we figure out what is going on and things quiet down around here, I'd want to be armed if I were you."

"Honestly?" He could hardly believe he was hearing a cop tell a civilian to carry a gun.

"You had to be trained to get that permit in the first place, and I know you're level-headed, so, yes." She smiled wryly. "Just don't shoot the good guys, okay?"

"Telling them apart from the bad ones can be tricky. How do you do it?"

"With training, discernment and a whole lot of prayer," she answered.

Noah was pleased. This side of Emily was more like what he remembered from years ago.

Even though he knew it would hurt to move his injured arm, he reached out with that hand and laid it over hers where she had rested it on the table.

When she looked into his eyes and he saw unshed tears, he merely said, "Amen."

Chief Rowlings made the decision to send Noah to the ER in a patrol car rather than the ambulance.

Emily realized she couldn't change fast enough to go on duty and step in as his escort, so she did the next best thing. She reported for work early and got permission to take one of the cars to the hospital without waiting for her partner.

Noah was still in the ER, sitting on the edge of a gurney, when she arrived. He looked a lot better than he had.

She couldn't help grinning. "Hey, you have color back in your cheeks."

"Oh, yeah?" He eyed the bandage on his bicep. "Maybe because they sewed me up."

"Stitches? How many?"

"I didn't count. Couldn't feel much after they gave me a shot. I'm not looking forward to the anesthetic wearing off, though."

"The chief says I can drive you home whenever you're ready to go."

"My car is still at your place. You can take me there."

"Only if the ER doc okays you to drive," Emily countered. "I don't want to be responsible for any accidents."

"Like my arm, you mean?"

"Low blow, but I deserved it," she admitted. "Of course you didn't have to listen to me when I told you to chase the guy."

"You have such a forceful way of asking, I didn't dare ignore you." There was a pause before he went on. "That's new. You used to be…"

"What? Nicer?"

"Hey, don't take offense. I was going to say, more easygoing."

"Sorry." Emily was penitent. "All cops catch a lot of flack on the job. I guess I assumed you were complaining, too."

"No. Not complaining," Noah said. "I understand you're a different person than you used to be because it's necessary. I just miss the old Emily."

"*I'm* different? What about you? I never thought I'd see you going to bat for criminals after law enforcement officers like me risk their lives to get them off the streets."

"You've never made a mistake? Arrested the wrong person? Look at what your partner almost did to me at the park. I was totally innocent. Did you want me to go to trial without adequate defense?"

"You weren't going to go to trial." *Why is he so stubborn?*

Noah's expression darkened, his eyes narrowing. "Who do you think came after *you* today?"

"Could have been anybody," Emily said, as much to convince herself as to convince Noah. However, when he brought up the shooting in the park, it gave her the shivers.

"Suppose that gunman who shot at us last night had had better aim? I'd take more precautions if I were you."

"You mean this?" She slapped the leather holster at her waist. "I'm even armed when I go jogging. I'd taken off my holster when I got home or I'd have been ready then, too."

"You can't wear that 24/7."

"I think you ought to worry more about yourself than about me. Did you get in touch with the guy who talked you into going to the park where the murder took place?"

"I did. At breakfast." Noah's shoulders slumped visibly. "I was going to bring him with me this morning to talk to you, but he ducked out the back of the restaurant and split."

"That's what you were doing at my place? I'd wondered."

"I wanted to learn more about the murders you mentioned. If it is a serial killer, I think you should bring in the FBI."

"That's totally up to my chief," Emily countered, secretly glad she didn't have to make command decisions. "Between you and me, I think so, too."

"Where did the other killings take place? Here in Paradise or somewhere else? That may make a difference."

"The bodies ended up here, and this last one definitely occurred on location in the park. Unless somebody finds murder sites elsewhere, they're all considered to have happened here. That's why the investigation is currently contained."

"I see." Shifting, Noah winced. "Would you mind asking somebody if I can leave so we can get going while my arm is kind of numb? I have work to do at the office."

"You may not feel up to that today."

"Doesn't matter how I feel. Clients won't wait. I promised Max, and I intend to do my job."

"Well," Emily said, feeling her smile starting to return, "one thing has stayed the same."

"What would that be?"

"Your stubbornness. You always were hardheaded, even when we were younger."

"I'll take that as a compliment," Noah said. "And you should take my opinion of you the same way. It's good to see you being forthright and standing up for your principles."

Emily was ready to agree and forgive him until he added, "Even if you are dead wrong sometimes."

She chose to make light of the comment by saying, "I don't mind being wrong once in a while, but I do not want to make a mistake that leaves me *dead* wrong, if you don't mind."

Noah gaped. "You must know I didn't mean anything of the kind."

"I do. Sit tight. I'll go see if I can talk a doctor into letting you go."

"Need a good lawyer to argue my case for you? I happen to know one."

"Oh, yeah? Last I heard, Max Maxwell was in here, too. While we're at it, we can swing by his room for a visit if you want."

"Now, that's a good idea," Noah said. "I'd call his cell and ask if he's up to it, but you stole my phone."

"Sorry."

Although she made a show of patting her pockets, Noah figured she'd left it behind. "Since we're going back for my car anyway, you can give it to me then, providing you didn't lose it."

"It's at the station. I assume you won't mind if we have it checked for activity last night."

"I'm surprised you didn't ask for it at the park," Noah said. "Apparently your chief really does believe I'm innocent."

"He does. I think you are, too. You should be happy to provide proof to strengthen that assumption."

"I am. No problem," Noah said. "Go get a doctor's release and ask about visiting Max. I'll be right here, aching and blaming you." He had to laugh when he saw Emily's expression. "Just kidding, honest."

"You'd better be."

Am I joking? Noah asked himself as she parted the curtains around the treatment cubicle and left. His immediate reaction when he'd thought she needed his help had been more instinctive than logical. For some reason, seeing her again had been affecting his normally thoughtful manner, and he was feeling as if they'd been transported ten years into the past and were the kind of buddies they'd once been. They'd looked out for each other back then, hadn't they?

College had made the difference, as he had expected it to. Except for casual friends, he had no ties to Paradise other than Max, who had urged him to leave for his own good. Until now it hadn't occurred to him that he had missed anybody else.

Now that he'd seen Emily Zwalt again, however, he knew better. He just wished she had remained the same sweet girl of his fond memories instead of becoming such a hard-bitten cop.

It tickled Emily when Noah's attending physician insisted he be in a wheelchair until he left the hospital. And, given his arm injury and sling, he needed to be pushed. When he argued, as she'd expected, she teased him. "Don't be silly. All you'd do is go around in circles with one arm out of commission."

She saw his frown when he looked up at her and said, "You're actually enjoying this, aren't you?"

"Not your injury, no." Her smile widened. "But it is fun to push you around, in more ways than one."

"Candid again, aren't you?"

"You said you liked it." Looking down at the top of his head as she pushed the chair down the hallway, she imagined him grinning. At least, she hoped he was. Over the years, she'd learned to counter serious emotions with humor, and if there ever was a reason for her to be somber, this was it. Noah had been injured because of her. That must never happen again. Never. As soon as they had visited his mentor, she'd take him to pick up his car and that would be that, except for the rare times when their jobs intersected.

Given Noah's plans to stay in Paradise only as long as Max needed his help, she figured the smartest thing she could do was tamp down any latent feelings of affection toward him and pretend she didn't love having him around. It had been a long time since she'd traded witty barbs with anyone the way she could with Noah. So long, in fact, that she'd forgotten how much she enjoyed it.

As they waited for the elevator, Emily fought feelings that kept insisting she should let herself accept Noah as he was and simply revel in the things they had in common rather than keep dredging up their differences.

A slow shake of her head and a sigh preceded the opening swish of the elevator doors. She had to bend down and brace herself to maneuver the wheelchair over the threshold, and that brought her cheek closer to Noah's, almost brushing against his ear, as she breathed deeply of his essence.

Time halted. If he turned his head just a little, her lips would have touched his cheek. But he didn't.

The chair bumped over the metal grooves, and Emily

straightened. Got control of her imagination. Spun him to face the front and pushed the button for the fifth floor.

Her head tilted up and her gaze traveled Heavenward as she sent up a silent prayer, unsure what words to use and leaving that up to the Lord.

Tears blurred her vision. She sniffled, glad Noah was facing away from her so he couldn't see her unacceptable behavior. The previous twenty-four hours had been especially stressful, so it was no wonder she was feeling off-balance and overwrought. Nobody was immune to stress, not even someone like her who trusted God and was secure in her chosen career.

That was the key, wasn't it? She was here, now, for a reason, and no matter how hard it was to cope, she wasn't in this alone. Faith would carry her through. It always had.

The only element that bothered her was having Noah in the picture. *Please, Father, protect him. Nobody but You knows how important he is to me.*

Heartfelt as it was, that prayer took her aback, because it forced her to acknowledge an emotional attachment to a man who obviously viewed her as a casual friend and no more. That was best for him, of course. So was his plan to leave Paradise as soon as possible, a detail that settled in her mind and caused her to add, *Send him away quickly, Lord, for his sake.*

Mentally, Emily meant the prayer 100 percent. Emotionally, she found herself sensing a deep loss despite the fact that he was currently close enough to touch.

The elevator stopped. The doors swished open. It was all she could do to stop herself from placing a whisper of a goodbye kiss on his dark hair as she once again bent over him to maneuver the wheelchair.

FIVE

"It's this way," Noah said, pointing with his good arm.

"You've visited him here before?"

"Of course. His speech is a little slow, but thankfully he's as sharp as ever."

"I'm glad. It must be very hard for him to be kept out of the office."

"It is." Noah gestured at an open door. "Here we are."

It was hard to imagine a vital man like Max being sidelined, and Noah was determined to keep his spirits up by sharing cases and asking for advice whether he actually needed it or not.

The gray-haired, wiry gentleman lawyer was propped up in bed and began to grin as soon as he saw he had visitors.

Noah hailed him and grinned. "Hello, Boss. You behaving yourself?"

Obviously delighted, Max nodded.

It was difficult to ignore the older man's lopsided smile, but it did seem to be evening out as the days passed.

"Closer, please," Noah told Emily with a sweep of his good arm. Max's brow furrowed and he looked quizzical, so Noah explained briefly. "I zigged when I should have zagged. It's not serious. Hospital protocol insisted I ride around, and Officer Zwalt was kind enough to push me."

"I was tricked into it," Emily gibed, surprising and pleasing Noah.

"She owed me," Noah said. He displayed his bandaged bicep. "This was her fault."

Max managed to comment. "Will you need…time off?"

"Nope. Not a minute," Noah replied. "I'm good to go. Which reminds me, remember that new pro bono case, Buddy Corrigan?"

Max nodded. "Yes. Did he hurt you?"

That was an interesting question, one Noah had asked himself prior to deciding against it. "I don't think so, Boss. Buddy's caused plenty of trouble, but the guy who did this was bigger, heavier. It happened when I stopped by Emily's house to talk to her about last night."

It amused Noah to see one of Max's bushy eyebrows twitch, and he chuckled. "Strictly business. I promise you. Let us fill you in. It turns out there's a good chance a serial killer of young women is operating in Paradise." Pausing, he looked to Emily. "Would you care to explain? I want him to hear the story from an original source."

"Of course." Rounding his wheelchair, she rested a hip on the edge of the high bed. Noah didn't understand until he saw her adjust her holster and realized she was sitting that way to keep the gun free. It hadn't occurred to him that she considered herself on duty, but it made sense. The uniform should have tipped him off right away. Instead, he'd assumed she was there simply to see him. What an idiot he was.

While Emily told the ailing lawyer about the recent murders of three young blonde women, Noah listened quietly until she began mentioning names. "Wait! What?"

She looked confused. "What?"

"Those names. Say them again."

"Charity Roskov was the latest victim. She's the one you found. Annie Hackett was last week's, and the week before that was Kit Lovell. Do they mean anything to you?""

Noah was glad he was already sitting down. "Yes, except for one thing. The victim last night was a blonde, and that doesn't fit. The Charity Roskov I know has dark hair. At least, she did when I spoke with her at the office. If that was her, I didn't make the connection." He raised a hand as if taking an oath. "I promise I didn't know. It was dark, and I wasn't expecting to see her again, especially not like that."

"What did you two talk about?"

"She wanted an order of protection because she was scared of her ex, Sam Fielding. I passed the work on to Stephanie. She's subbing for her aunt, Olivia Brooks. Normally Olivia would handle that kind of paperwork, but Stephanie seems capable."

"A piece of paper never was a good way to stay safe from attack," Emily told him. "Even if a judge had had time to rule on it, it's still just a suggestion. How many cruel men do you know who would pay attention to it?"

Max had tears in his eyes. "Olivia has been here with me most of the time," he said softly. "I'm so...sorry."

"It's not your fault," Emily said quickly. "Whoever is doing this to innocent women has been at it for weeks."

Noah spoke up to stop her. "Max's problems started several weeks ago."

Speaking his thoughts for him, Emily said, "That's when you came back here to work?"

"You can't possibly think I'm responsible."

"I didn't say that, but think for a minute. Max gets sick, and you come to Paradise to help out at the very time somebody decides to murder blonde women and dump them here. What are the chances of that being a coincidence?"

"Great, actually. The trip happened on such short notice, almost no one knew I was coming. Besides, the victims you mentioned were on the periphery of my life, at best."

"Nevertheless, I think you should speak with Chief Rowlings and help us figure this out."

Noah agreed, in principle. What bothered him was the look Emily had sent him when he'd admitted to recognizing the names and realized he'd failed to identify a person he should have known on sight. In retrospect, he had had an inkling of something odd but had discounted the feeling when logic had taken over. There was no reason for him to consider that the victim had altered her appearance, although it did make sense if she was truly fearful and in hiding.

The pieces of this puzzle that failed to fit, however, were gigantic. First, there was Buddy's phone call summoning him to the gazebo. Then there was the way he'd ducked out of the diner and disappeared. That hardly indicated innocence, did it? Plus, outside of the brief office visit, Noah didn't know the Roskov woman and was barely acquainted with Annie Hackett, other than a couple of dates in grad school.

And Kit? He wasn't even sure Lovell was her last name, but given the description, he assumed it must be her. She'd been a pretty waitress at his favorite café on campus, and they'd flirted a little. Everybody did, since Kit was a naturally friendly person.

"One question," Noah said, concentrating on Emily's face in the hopes he could read her mood and would find it favorable. "I'm not sure about Kit's last name. What did she do for a living?"

With a tilt of her head, Emily stared back at him. "She put herself through college as a waitress, but she was working as an executive assistant when she was killed."

"When was she a waitress? Where? Tell me it wasn't near Kansas State."

"As a matter of fact, it was," Emily told him. She stood and took control of the wheelchair. "Excuse us, please, Mr. Maxwell. Noah needs to be debriefed ASAP if we intend to put a halt to this killing spree."

"It *can't* be connected to me," he argued all the way to the elevator.

"Then help us prove it," Emily countered. "You have nothing to hide, right?"

"Right." Noah knew he was innocent without a doubt. The way he saw it, his biggest challenge was making sure he wasn't the only one who thought so.

Once they were out of the hospital, Emily set the brake on the chair and circled to face Noah. "Here's what's going to happen. My unit is parked right over there. I'll drive it under the portico and pick you up so we can leave the wheelchair here."

"No."

She could hardly believe he was arguing. "Why not?"

"Because I can walk. And I don't relish sitting here in the open, waiting for you."

Noting the way he was scanning the parking lot, Emily nodded. "For once, you're right."

She offered her arm. Noah ignored it, kicked the footrests out of the way and stood. To her delight, his balance seemed normal, and he didn't act as if the blood loss had made him weak. Nevertheless, she stayed at his elbow as they walked to her patrol car, just in case he faltered. He didn't.

Unlocking the doors remotely, she gestured. "In you go."

Noah was still trying to fasten his seat belt when she slid behind the wheel. "Let me get that for you?"

"I am not an invalid," he snapped.

"Fine. If it takes you too long, we can order a pizza delivered."

"Very funny."

"I thought so." Rather than continue to argue, she simply guided the other end of the buckle and held it steady until she heard a click. Perspiration on Noah's forehead was proof of the effort he'd had to make, and that upset her. "You don't have to prove anything to me, you know."

He huffed. "Maybe not, but I have plenty to prove to myself. I can't sit back and nurse my wound while Max's law practice falls apart."

"Of course you can't." Changing the subject on purpose as she drove through town, she said, "The chief is going to want details of your connections to our victims, plus anything else you can think of that might help. You're a lawyer. You know what I mean."

"You can't expect me to remember a date I went on probably three years ago. Annie was a sweet kid but not all that memorable, I'm afraid. And I never did get around to dating Kit."

"But you thought about it."

"Well, sure. She was a flirt. Of course it occurred to me to ask her out."

The muscles in Emily's neck and shoulders tightened, and her hands fisted the steering wheel. Astonishingly, she recognized a jolt of jealousy. That did not please her one bit, nor was she going to allow it to continue.

Shrugging and flexing her fingers, she wished her seat belt allowed the kind of unrestrained movement necessary to stretch properly. “Just do the best you can, and we’ll take it from there. How about other friends from your past? Do any of them resemble the blue-eyed blondes we already know about?”

A sidelong glance told her he’d closed his eyes. When he opened them, looked over at her and said, “No, the others mostly looked like you,” Emily hoped she’d managed to hide her visceral reaction.

“Don’t look so surprised,” Noah said. “I always did think you were the prettiest girl in town.”

“Oh, yeah, right.”

“I mean it.”

“You had me fooled. I never caught the slightest glimmer of interest.”

“Which turned out to be just as well,” he replied softly. “The people we became are definitely not compatible.”

The truth of his assessment didn’t do much to soften the statement, but it did help her handle the emotional impact of hearing that he’d once thought she was attractive.

“Wow, that’s the second time today you’ve been right,” she teased. “I may need to make notes to keep track.”

“You know I’ll be glad to keep reminding you,” Noah said, smiling slightly.

“I have no doubt.”

What she wanted to ask next was personal, but she figured if she kept it casual enough, he wouldn’t take the question too seriously. It was worth a try.

“So,” Emily drawled, “if you thought I was pretty, why didn’t you ever ask me out?”

"You always had plenty of boyfriends. Besides, I knew I was leaving for college. It wouldn't have been fair to you."

"Very noble of you." It took every ounce of self-control to keep from squeezing the steering wheel so hard her hands hurt. She didn't like the visceral reaction, but deep in her heart, she knew he'd done the right thing—for both of them.

She heard him sigh. "Actually, I figured you'd be married and have a couple of kids by now."

"I almost was."

"Almost?" She could feel his probing gaze without looking.

"It didn't work out," was all she could manage without risking the tears that usually followed the telling of her sad story.

When Noah said, "I'm sorry," Emily could tell he truly meant it, and that was almost enough to make her cry anyway.

"It was a long time ago."

"I could always have a friendly talk with him. You know, convince him he'd made a mistake, if that's what you want."

"No."

"I'm serious, Em. If I learned anything in law school, it was how to convince people. I'd be glad to intercede on your behalf. After all, you did save my life last night at the park when you knocked me out of the line of fire."

"Just drop it, Noah."

"Come on. Give me a chance."

Pulling the patrol car into the parking lot at the police station, Emily turned off the engine, swiveled, and stared at him. "There are no more chances for Jake, or for me. He's dead."

SIX

Noah was floored. What could he say? How could he help her? Finally, he found his voice. "Would you like to talk about it?"

Silence reigned inside the patrol car while normal life continued outside. Although Emily was shaking her head, she began to speak, her words barely audible. "Jake was a cop."

Because she stopped talking, Noah asked, "You met that way?"

"No. It was after…that I decided to go to the police academy." Emily sniffed and raised her chin as if strengthening her resolve. "I wanted to carry on the work he'd begun as a way to honor his memory." Another long pause. "I know I can never replace Jake—nobody can—but at least I can help put criminals behind bars."

"The guilty deserve to be held accountable." Noah agreed.

"But a lot of times they're not," Emily said. When she looked over at him with her brow furrowed and her gaze locking on his, Noah grew decidedly uncomfortable. Given the conversations they'd had recently, he wasn't surprised when she added, "Slick lawyers get them off all the time."

"My goal is to defend the wrongly accused."

"Very commendable. Tell that to Jake's parents. The guy who ambushed him had been in jail, until somebody in Little Rock got the charges against him dropped."

"I'm truly sorry," Noah told her, "but you can't hold one mistake against all attorneys."

Emily broke eye contact with him and turned to stare out the window of the police car. "I'll stop doing that as soon as you stop assuming that police officers like me are on a crusade to arrest innocent people."

"I never said that."

"You imply it every time you take a criminal case." She opened the driver's door and got out, adjusting her duty belt and holster. "Come on. Chief Rowlings will want to know everything you can remember about your former friends, especially the blonde ones."

"There's really not a lot to tell," Noah said, joining her. "It's not like I keep a little black book of women's names and numbers."

Emily had her back to him and was keying in an entry code at the locked rear door of the station. She stepped back and held the door open for him to pass, so he did. The way Noah saw it, his former friend had a hardened heart, and the fewer waves he made, the better. Not that he didn't understand why she was bitter. A criminal had stolen the happy future she'd imagined and had done it with the help of the courts. Mistakes were made every day because people were fallible. No one could hope to guarantee perfect justice all the time. Not judges, not attorneys, not even police officers. All any of them could do was their best in a given situation, which was exactly what he was doing now.

Following Emily's directions, Noah passed through

a narrow corridor between banks of cells. Most were empty.

"I was hoping you'd picked up Buddy Corrigan," he said over his shoulder.

"We're looking. No sign of him yet. Any chance he was the assailant who knifed you?"

"Not unless he can fly," Noah replied. "I don't think he could have gotten across town to your place that fast on foot after he ditched me, although nothing is impossible if he had a car stashed. Did your people find anything on closed circuit cameras?"

"Still checking," she said flatly.

"I'm looking forward to results."

"Which you will only see if we need you to ID your client," Emily warned. "As the victim of a crime, you know we won't be showing you pictures of suspects until we're sure."

"What about professional courtesy?"

She huffed. "That, Mr. Holden, is an oxymoron as far as I'm concerned."

"You mean as far as *I'm* concerned, don't you?"

Instead of answering, Emily knocked on a closed door, then opened it slightly. "I have Noah Holden with me, Chief," she announced. "Where do you want me to put him?"

Several wry but amusing answers popped into Noah's mind and were almost funny enough to make him smile. He squelched the urge. This interview was no laughing matter. Rowlings didn't know him nearly as well as Max did and could conceivably suspect him if he didn't choose his words carefully. This was murky ground he was treading, and caution was advised.

Invited in, he offered his good hand, shook with the

chief and settled into the chair closest to the front of the desk.

"Good to hear it wasn't serious." Rowlings indicated the bandage and sling with a lift of his chin. "How are you feeling? Sore?"

"A little. It's probably going to leave a bigger scar on my pride than it will on my arm."

The chief chuckled. "Probably. What caused the confrontation in the first place? How did you come in contact with the perp?"

Noah didn't want to throw Emily under the bus to salve his own ego, so he simply said, "Wrong place, wrong time."

"What brought you to Officer Zwalt's house?"

"A whim," Noah said with a sigh. "I'd been planning to haul Corrigan over there and make him explain why he'd phoned me to come to the park. When he gave me the slip, I decided to drop by anyway."

"Do you and Emily have a history?"

"In a manner of speaking," Noah said, fully conscious of her presence behind him. "We knew each other back in the day. Went to the same high school, although I was a couple of years ahead of her."

"I see. Nothing more?"

Noah felt his cheeks warming. "No, sir. Just friends."

"Okay. I'm going to have you interviewed by a different officer anyway." Looking past Noah, he focused on Emily. "Nothing personal, Zwalt. Who do we have who isn't a childhood friend?"

"That's hard to say in a small town like Paradise," she replied. "The only one I can think of is Cal Dodge. He's pretty green, though."

"Granted. A simple interview like this one will be good training for him. Set it up." Rowlings stood to offer his hand to Noah again. "Thanks for coming in so promptly."

"I'd say it's my pleasure, but in this instance, it isn't. I don't like hearing that there may be a connection between me and your murder victims."

"Coincidences do happen," the chief drawled. "Don't worry about a thing. We'll have it sorted out soon."

Noah wanted to express hope that the chief was right but chose to merely nod in agreement. Putting those victims together and placing them in his life, however tenuously, had shaken him. There couldn't be a connection. There simply couldn't be. But what other explanation fit? Did someone have a grudge against the local police? Or was a disgruntled client trying to discredit him in order to harm Max's law practice? That notion was farfetched but made about as much sense as thinking a killer was trying to frame him personally.

"I don't think I have this kind of dedicated enemies," Noah told the chief in parting. "I'm looking forward to helping you put the pieces of the puzzle together."

"God willing, before anybody else dies," Rowlings added soberly.

Noah nodded, whispering, "Amen," as he followed Emily from the room.

Listening in on Noah's interview told Emily nothing she didn't already know. If Noah did have a connection to the initial victims, it was tenuous. The most recent murder, however, was different. He had talked to the Roskov woman within hours of her death, so his name had to remain on the list of possible suspects. She smiled. *Person of interest* was now the official title, but as far as she was concerned, there was nothing wrong with calling them what they were—suspects.

Noah's earlier questions had caused her to focus on losing Jake when she'd been convinced she was long past that pain. Perhaps she never really would heal. That wasn't all bad, was it? The more she remembered her former fiancé, the better she'd remember why she'd taken on this job and what her God-given task was.

She joined Noah in the hallway as soon as Cal finished the interview. "I've been told to drive you back to your car."

"You don't have to sound so unhappy about it."

"Just doing my job."

"Right." He gestured with his good arm. "Lead on."

They were settled in a patrol car and passing through town when Noah said, "Me, too."

"You too what?"

"Just doing my job. To the best of my ability. The same as you are."

"I never said you weren't. I just don't like to see somebody bend the law to get what they want."

The angry expression Emily glimpsed gave Noah an edge of danger that made him look even more handsome—a fact that she categorically denied.

"I never bend anything," he stated. "I take advantage of opportunities to give my clients second chances, to allow them to return to the lives they once had, to help them find the same happiness we all seek, even if they have made mistakes."

"Yeah, well, I've seen the results of too much forgiveness. It can be lethal."

"That's the problem, isn't it?" Noah asked. "You can't forgive the man who took somebody you loved, and you don't dare blame God, so you're taking it out on me."

"I'm doing nothing of the kind."

"Ha!"

Emily was searching for the best rebuttal when her radio squealed. "All units." Dispatch gave the ten-code for a possible attack in progress, and Emily was quick to decide. "Unit three is one block away. Responding."

"Copy. Ambulance ETA five."

"What's going on?" Noah began bracing himself.

The glance she gave him was meant to be dismissive. "Domestic abuse."

"What are you getting me into now?"

"Nothing that concerns you. A life may be at stake, so hang on, Mr. Holden. We're going for a little ride."

Acceleration pinned him to the seat. Emily's hands gripped the steering wheel. She knew she was breaking rules by answering this call with a civilian on board, but the other units had reported extended ETAs, and her unit was practically on top of the incident. If she ended up being disciplined, fine. Saving a life meant more than preserving her rank.

A crowd had gathered in front of the address dispatch had given. Many of the bystanders were pointing at the porch, and more than one person was snapping photos with a cell phone.

Emily slid to a stop at the curb, shouted at Noah, "Stay in the car," then hit the ground running. Her palm rested on the grip of her gun.

"He's long gone," someone yelled. "Call an ambulance."

"We have one on the way," Emily shouted. "What happened here?" As she spoke, she was climbing the porch stairs, still wary because she had no official backup yet. A young woman lay prostrate in front of the open door. Emily felt for a carotid pulse and felt it, so she rolled the victim over and began CPR.

By the third chest compression, her hands were

covered in blood, and she figured her efforts were futile, but she didn't stop until the paramedics arrived. Rocking back on her heels to make room for them, she gasped to catch her breath.

The medics worked rapidly, assessed the victim, loaded her on a gurney and sped away, lights flashing, siren wailing.

Fighting tears brought on by exhaustion and a fear of failure, Emily stood and addressed the crowd. "Everyone please remain here until we can get your names."

When someone handed her a clean towel, she realized her hands were shaking. Another person provided a container of sanitizing wipes. Other units had arrived, and fellow officers were forming a loose line around the observers, herding them into a tighter group to be interviewed on scene.

Noah stood apart from the rest. His face was pale and his jaw agape. As he approached, Emily could tell he was feeling strong emotions.

She descended to the lawn and faced him. "I told you to stay in the car."

"I needed to get a closer look," Noah said.

"This was a domestic," Emily told him. "No connection to the other cases." She noticed he seemed slightly unsteady. "Besides, you were with me when it happened."

Noah had paused at the foot of the stairs and rested one hand on the railing. "She's blonde and blue-eyed."

"I didn't notice her eye color," Emily said.

"I don't have to see it. I know who she is."

"One of your clients?"

Noah nodded. "Yes. Laura Bright. Husband's name is Jim."

"I'm sorry," Emily said, softening toward him, "but

we know who's responsible this time. There are plenty of witnesses."

"That doesn't make this any less tragic." Noah turned and touched her shoulder. "You did everything you could."

"I'm afraid it wasn't enough." She was slipping into self-condemnation when Noah said something that upset her so much she was speechless.

"You're not trained to do the impossible, Em. You're trained to do your best, to give it all you have to give and leave the results to God. Expecting more of yourself or arguing with the outcome will eventually destroy you."

She knew exactly what he really meant and who he was referring to. This wasn't a speech about the poor victim she'd found on the porch. It was Noah's way of reminding her she wasn't in charge of the events in her life any more than she could change the fact that CPR may not have been enough this time.

Emily understood that better than anybody imagined. She'd watched and prayed and wept in disbelief as the most valiant efforts at resuscitation had failed to save her beloved Jake.

Gaping at Noah, she wanted to rail at him for being insensitive, but she couldn't. Why?

Because he was right.

SEVEN

Noah's wound ached, and fatigue was increasing, yet he didn't want to leave Emily when she was feeling so down, even if that emotional reaction was illogical. Nothing much made sense since they'd met again after so many years. Unfortunately, rationalizing did little to alleviate his concern.

"Why don't we check with the hospital in a little while and ask about my client's condition?" Noah suggested.

"What do you mean, *we*?"

"Okay then, you, although I am her attorney of record."

"You *were*."

"Not necessarily past tense. The medics must have thought she had a chance or they wouldn't have transported her so fast."

Noah saw Emily arch her brows as if slightly surprised before conceding, "You may have a point. I'll drop you at your car and..."

"I want to stay with you."

"There's no need for that. I'll let you know if your client survived to pay her bill."

"Low blow, Officer Zwalt," Noah said, reverting to a more professional approach to hide the hurt.

"I'm really sorry. It's been a lousy morning."

Seeing how truly penitent she was made it easier to forgive her. "Yeah, I noticed." Supporting his arm in addition to the sling, he started back for the police car. A sense of her presence told him Emily was following.

After she got in and had helped him secure his seat belt again, she rested her hands on the wheel. "I'll need to go home and change into a clean uniform, anyway, so you may as well pick up your car. After that, I can't stop you from going to the hospital or anywhere else. I do advise against wearing yourself out, though. You are injured."

"That I am. How long do you expect to be?"

"At home? Not long. I'll inform the chief I'm temporarily out of service and explain why. If he doesn't need me elsewhere, I'll visit this victim later. Assuming she's still with us."

Noah nodded. "I have a strong feeling she will be. I don't know why. I just do."

"I hope you're right," Emily said, pulling into traffic. "It would be nice to save *one* once in a while, know what I mean?"

"I do. Think of what it feels like for me to keep learning that my prior acquaintances are meeting horrible ends."

Nodding while keeping her eyes on traffic, Emily said, "Not to mention how that looks to people like me. If you were a stranger with no history in Paradise and didn't have Max to vouch for you, there's a good chance you'd be in police custody right now."

"That sounds like a conversation we've already had,"

Noah remarked. "What happened to 'innocent until proven guilty'?"

It surprised him to see her almost smile. "If you ask me, that should be worded differently. I'd say, 'Under surveillance until shown to be innocent,' instead."

"You can't prove a negative, Em."

"Maybe not, but I can uncover whoever is really guilty and make sure they pay."

Noah started to shrug. The pain made him wince. Experience had shown there was no point in arguing. He and Emily should have been cooperating and supporting each other, yet they were as opposed as two sides in a fighting war.

Now that she'd told him about her personal loss, he could better commiserate but that wasn't enough to change his own mind. He'd come to the rescue of many poor souls whose mistakes had landed them in jail despite extenuating circumstances. Parents had stolen food to feed starving children. Mates had been separated through misunderstandings and had caused problems over differences that should have been arbitrated and resolved. Workers had been unfairly blamed for the acts of others. The list went on and on.

And in this case? His thoughts drifted back to the woman on the porch, and he prayed she'd survive to corroborate or refute the testimony of all those so-called witnesses. He'd seen mob mentality at work before, and unless someone reliable had seen her husband actually injure her, there was a chance he was innocent.

That was the kind of out-of-the-box thinking Emily failed to comprehend, Noah concluded. To her, life was cut-and-dried with little wiggle room. To him, innocence was as clear as the bandage on his arm. All one had to do was look for it to see it.

And be open to recognizing it when it presented itself, he added. Like his own case. He figured it would be wise to call his old office and ask for copies of the records of his official activities from before he'd come to Paradise. Even if the police never asked to see them, he might spot a clue.

"My cell phone," Noah reminded her. "I'll need it back."

"I turned it in at the station this morning when I picked up this car."

"Terrific. So you're holding it hostage?"

Emily chuckled. "In a manner of speaking. I'll see what I can do to get it released. Why don't you buy a burner phone until I do?"

"I'd feel like a spy or a drug dealer using one of those throwaways," Noah said, sending her a wry look. "Besides, my phone has all my contacts programmed into it."

"Understood. I'll speak to the chief." Emily was gliding to a stop at the curb in front of her house. There was yellow crime scene tape strung across her porch and side yard.

She shivered. "It feels ominous seeing all that tape."

"Yeah, it is off-putting. Is it okay for me to take my car since it's parked on the outside?"

"Sure. Have at it. Just drive carefully, okay?"

"Always." Pausing on the sidewalk, Noah waved with his good arm. "You be careful, too."

Emily didn't break stride but she did call back, "Always."

She had her house key ready to insert in the lock, reached out—and saw that the door was ajar.

One second she was weary, the next on full alert.

Remaining on the porch, she drew her sidearm and held it ready while phoning 911 and reporting a possible break-in.

"That's right. I normally lock up, but there's been a lot of distraction here. Stand by while I check the scene."

Swiveling through the open door, she gripped her pistol in a shooter's stance to scan the room. Nothing looked out of place. The kitchen was open to view from there and empty, so she headed for the hallway next. Bedroom doors were closed. She gave the first one a push and listened as it hit the rubber stopper on the wall, then gave the room a quick scan. Nothing. No one.

Too soon to relax, Emily told herself. She checked the small bathroom. Unoccupied. One more room to go.

The old house always creaked and groaned, especially during weather changes, and this day was no different. The trick was to separate normal sounds from strange ones. Was that a dull thud? Were there going to be more sounds in a cadence, like footsteps? What about that squeak the windows made when they were raised or lowered?

Emily's hand closed on the knob as she realized something vital. Living alone, she never closed her bedroom door, and it was presently shut tight.

Taking a firm grip she tried to enter. The door didn't budge. Someone must have locked it!

Intent on drawing any prowler's attention to the interior, she made a fist, banged on the door and shouted, "Open up! Police!" then spun on her heel and raced to the kitchen door because it was closest.

Bursting into the yard, she followed the same path she'd used when pursuing the man who had knifed Noah and, again, hesitated before swinging around the blind corner.

A dark shape whizzed past her in a blur.

"Halt!"

The figure half turned and lashed out. A blade flashed in the sunlight. Emily fell back, her gun raised. There was only a millisecond in which to decide whether or not to fire before the fleeing prowler kicked out and connected with one of her knees, dropping her in her tracks before disappearing over the neighbor's board fence.

Angry, frustrated and more than a little embarrassed, Emily stayed down, pressed her back to the wall so no one could get behind her, and started to call for more backup. Her phone was in her hand when she caught movement out of the corner of her eye.

She whipped the gun into firing position. Aimed. And recognized Noah.

He raised his hands, even the one hindered by the sling. "Don't shoot!"

"What are you doing here?"

"I looked in my mirror and saw you stop at your front door and pull your gun, so I backed up to see what was wrong. What happened this time?"

"I surprised a prowler."

"Which way did he go?"

"Never mind. You chased one perp for me, and look what it got you. Stay right here where I can see you while I report and get some backup."

Noah held out a hand of assistance.

Emily considered not taking it but gave in. Her aching knee was probably going to swell, so the sooner she got herself up off the ground and iced it, the better.

"You're limping," he remarked with a scowl.

"Twisted my knee," she alibied. Making sure her gear was in place and holstering the pistol, she finished phoning her station, explained what had happened since her initial standby call, and let Noah help her up the stairs into the kitchen.

"Ice would be good," Emily said, partly because she wanted it and partly to give him something useful to do.

He wrapped some cubes in a kitchen towel, handed the bundle to her and stepped back. "Anything else?"

"Yes. Go watch for the incoming units and be sure to look innocent when you let them in so they don't cuff you."

"Very funny. They should be used to me by now. I've turned up on nearly everything you've been involved in for the last twenty-four."

Feeling throbbing pain and not wanting to show it, she shooed him off. "Let me process all this, will you? I know I'm going to be kidded something awful when my unit finds out."

"Why didn't you shoot?" Noah asked.

Suspecting that part of her hesitation stemmed from his influence, Emily just shrugged. "Happened too fast. She was on me before I had a chance to react."

Noah's brow knit. "She?"

That slip of the tongue had surprised Emily, too. "I did say *she*, didn't I? I don't know why. Maybe because the person who ran into me was small, wiry and very quick."

"Men can be like that, too."

Thinking, she pressed her lips together. "I know. There must have been something about the prowler that made me imagine a gender. The face was covered." Closing her eyes, she pictured the event, beginning with the rush by the corner and the swish of the knife cutting the air right in front of her.

Emily's eyes popped open, and she stared into the distance, not focusing on reality but on memory. The hand. It was the hand. Those slim fingers. That pale skin.

"The hand holding the knife looked female," she told Noah, getting excited. "That's what I recognized."

"No chance you're mistaken?"

She snorted a chuckle. "There is always a chance of that, as you like to remind me, but the more I think about it, the more positive I am."

"Okay." Acting uneasy, he gestured toward the front of the house. "I'll just go watch for backup, shall I?"

"Please."

Readjusting the makeshift ice pack over her knee, Emily heard the approach of her fellow officers and listened to Noah telling them what had happened and where she was. It didn't please her to see Calvin Dodge come running into the kitchen ahead of everyone else.

"Simmer down, Cal. The perp is gone." Emily smiled to try to calm him.

"We can't get one of the inside doors open," he blurted. "Want us to break it down?"

"No." She pointed to a peg next to the back door. "The master key is up there on a hook. The old-fashioned-looking one. That's it."

He was gone for barely half a minute when Noah appeared. "I think you should come with me," he said soberly.

"Now?"

"Now, if you think it's okay to walk." He was eyeing the ice pack. "It's important."

"Okay." Emily levered herself to her feet and rested a hand on his arm for support.

They worked their way through the cops bunched at her bedroom door and stopped. If she had been alone, she might have gasped when she recognized an object from her very own kitchen.

The black handle of a large carving knife was protruding from the center of her pillow. Right where she laid her head every night.

EIGHT

Once Emily's house had been processed for fingerprints and she was let back in, she quickly changed to a clean uniform. Noah figured she probably had an ulterior motive for accepting his offer to drive her to the hospital, but he didn't care as long as she went along with his advice and had her knee checked while they were there.

The local medical facility was larger than Paradise warranted because it served several adjoining counties as well. They entered via the emergency room doors.

Noah took one whiff and wished he could hold his breath indefinitely. The air inside the hospital had a distinctive bite to it, tangy with disinfectant and carrying an undercurrent of illness and despair. A couple of empty gurneys were parked along one wall, and there was muted conversation coming from a cubicle halfway to the indoor access to the main hospital. Lack of excitement or rapid action suggested that his injured client wasn't still there.

Hoping she hadn't already passed away, Noah asked at a nurse's station while Emily spoke with a physician's assistant about her knee.

"Mrs. Bright is in surgery," a nurse in green scrubs told him.

"I know she lost a lot of blood. What's the prognosis?"

"Are you a relative?"

He knew better than to claim he was, so he merely said, "I'm her attorney."

"Then I suggest you wait on the surgical floor."

"Thanks. Do you know if she's being guarded?"

The nurse started to shrug, then turned as the ambulance bay doors swung open to admit more emergency medics and a new patient. "Sorry. Gotta go. Third floor."

"Gotcha." With a sigh, Noah sought out Emily and found her emerging from one of the exam cubicles. "Laura's still in surgery but alive, so that's good news. What about your knee?"

"Ice and elevate it. I told you I didn't need to come here."

"Yeah, well… We can wait for Laura on three." He gestured toward a bank of elevators. "Shall we?"

"What did they tell you?"

"Nothing. You'll have better results because you're in uniform. I'm hoping we can talk to a doctor if we're in the right place when one comes by. It may be a while before she's out of the recovery room."

"You really did get the sense she's expected to survive?"

"I did."

Together they took an elevator. A uniformed Paradise police officer was waiting in the hallway when they got off. Noah greeted the man amiably and offered his hand while Emily merely nodded because she knew him.

"Steve Anderson," the young officer said to Noah before focusing on Emily. "What can you tell me about this case, Zwalt? All they said was to stick with Ms. Bright if she made it."

"We don't know a lot," Emily answered. "Witnesses

said her husband was involved, but he's in the wind. Until he's picked up, it's a good idea to keep watch on her room." She paused. "Were you up here when they wheeled her to surgery?"

"Yes, ma'am."

"Did she say anything? Anything at all?"

The younger cop fidgeted. "She was pretty out of it."

Noah lowered his voice to affect a calm he wasn't feeling. "Tell us. Please. All we know is what was said on the original 911 call. Laura and her husband had been arguing, and it got physical."

"I don't know anything about that," Anderson said. "Is the husband's name Jim?"

"Yes." Noah let his breath out in a noisy whoosh when the young cop continued. "She said somebody else knifed her. It wasn't Jim."

"You're positive?"

"Yes. She kept shaking her head when she spotted me and lifted the oxygen mask. She kept saying, 'No. Jimmy.'"

Emily sighed in disappointment. "And you think that meant he didn't hurt her? Sounds more like a repeat of what she must have said when he was attacking."

"That's what I thought at first, so I asked if he was the one who had hurt her."

"She actually said he wasn't?"

"Well, they pushed me away and put the mask back over her face, but it was clear plastic and she mouthed, *No*."

"Not enough," Emily said flatly. "Maybe Mr. Bright can shed more light on the situation once we have him in custody."

Noah interrupted. "Assuming he comes quietly. I'd hate to see him hurt, or worse, if he resists arrest."

"There are maybe a few incidents where things got out of hand, but by and large, people like me are just trying to keep the peace," Emily said. "When I took the oath to protect and serve the public, I meant it."

Noah held up a hand, palm toward both of the police officers. "I know that. I also know that fear or anger can make people do things they would never even consider under different circumstances. Take Jim Bright, for instance. When he took off, maybe he was just trying to distance himself from Laura to calm down, not running away because he'd harmed her. Have you thought of that?"

"You never give up, do you?" Body braced, knee throbbing, Emily faced him boldly.

"No more than you do," Noah replied. "I suggest we table this discussion until we've had a chance to interview Laura."

"She may still try to protect Jim by denying he harmed her. That kind of wrong thinking occurs all the time."

"That's where you and I come in," Noah said flatly. "It's up to us to separate the innocent from the guilty."

Emily set her jaw. "Wrong. It's up to a judge and jury to do that. Our job is to provide the tools they need to bring justice."

"Only if we can do it without prejudice," Noah argued. "That's the real key."

"Do you mean to say you're ready to forgive whoever is killing women you've come in contact with? What about the victims? Their grieving families?"

Instead of the capitulation Emily apparently expected, Noah said, "I like to think I could," endeavoring to leave her as convicted as she'd obviously intended him to be.

Perhaps the day would never come when she'd be able to forgive anybody for stealing Jake from her, but it was Noah's hope and prayer that she'd find enough peace to carry her through. To lift her up and comfort her when she relived that pain of loss, as she appeared to be doing right now.

When her glance met his, it created a bond that touched him so deeply he wasn't sure what to do. Part of him insisted he step back and give her more space while another part wanted to enfold her in a tender embrace.

Emily put a hand to her temple and swayed slightly. That did it. Noah reached out. "Are you feeling that hit in the head you got at the park?"

"No, I..."

She didn't resist when he slipped his good arm around her shoulders. The next thing he knew she was leaning into him, resting her cheek against his chest, and he could feel a sympathetic cadence of heartbeats.

"Is it your knee? Too much pain?"

"I'm fine. I just need a moment."

"What you need is some sleep and a decent meal," Noah said. "As soon as we find out when to expect Laura to be able to talk, I'm taking you down to the cafeteria."

Officer Anderson interrupted. "They told me at least two hours and that was—" he checked his watch "—less than an hour ago. You've got plenty of time. I'll keep watch up here."

Stepping aside to speak to the young officer, Noah reminded him, "Whoever did this, whether it was the spouse or not, is still at large. Stay alert. This is already a big mess, and I'd hate to see you added to the casualties."

Although neither officer looked pleased to hear his

advice, neither of them countered it. *That's because I'm right*, Noah thought. Not only were young blonde women falling victim to a killer, something else was going on involving Emily and perhaps even himself. Logically, since the deceased women had ties to him, however tenuous, it might mean that he was the link, although why that should affect Emily, a brunette, didn't compute.

Neither did Buddy's apparent attempt to frame him for one of the murders. That was assuming, of course, that the plea for help had actually come from that client. Destroying your pro bono attorney made no sense. So what were they missing? And why was some strange woman threatening Emily?

Recalling the shots at the park when he'd found the Roskov body, Noah became more and more certain that he hadn't been in the crosshairs. Emily had.

And by the looks of her bed pillow after this last incident, she still was.

"Feeling better?" Noah asked as they sipped iced tea at the end of their cafeteria meal.

Emily nodded. "I wasn't that hungry."

He chuckled. "If this was an example of how you eat when you're *not* hungry, I'd hate to see you when you're starving."

"Okay, okay. So I did need food. You win. This time. Just don't make it a habit."

"Has anybody ever told you you're too competitive?" Noah asked.

"A few times." *Like hundreds*, she added to herself. She jerked and almost spilled her iced tea when her radio sounded off. "Zwalt, are you still at the hospital?"

"Affirmative."

"Copy. You're wanted in the recovery room. The victim is conscious."

Noah was on his feet almost as quickly as she was, accompanied her to the elevator and stayed close. An excited Officer Anderson was waiting for them when they got off.

"They're about to move her to ICU, but they said you could talk to her," he blurted. "The chief wants you to do it instead of me."

"I'm going in too," Noah said.

Emily raised an eyebrow at him but didn't forbid it. Having someone with her who the woman knew might prove advantageous, and she figured she could always banish him if he got too pushy.

Dry erase boards mounted on the wall above narrow beds identified each occupant at a glance. Several nurses were tending to machinery around a different recovering patient, leaving Laura Bright temporarily alone except for a woman in a long white coat at her bedside.

Emily not only halted, she put out an arm to stop Noah. The pristine white physician's coat fit into the scenario fine, but the person standing next to Laura was also wearing ragged jeans and dirty athletic shoes.

"Who are you, and what are you doing?" Emily demanded, keeping her voice low yet firm.

The person by the patient said nothing.

Easing Noah to the side, Emily reached toward the white sleeve. "Back away. Now."

A very slight movement was the only indication that anything might happen right before the woman in white lowered her head, spun, and plowed directly into Emily, sending her staggering.

Noah lost his footing when she careened into him, hit

the elevated bed and fell to the floor. This time, when Emily landed on top of him, she was out of control and smashed against his injury.

He yowled. Nurses came running. Bedlam reigned. And the suspect in the dirty sneakers made a dash for the door.

By the time Emily had regained her feet, the uniformed officer from the hallway was coming through the swinging doors, hunched over and leaning against the jamb. Both hands were pressing against his stomach. His eyes were wide, his skin pale.

Limping, Emily sprinted after the escaping suspect. As she passed Anderson, he took one step forward and collapsed against her. Instinct helped her catch him before he hit the floor.

She gripped his arm to support him, knowing that if she let go he'd fall, and shouted at the nursing station through the partially open doorway. "Call security. Lock down the hospital. There's a killer loose in here!"

NINE

At first glance, Noah thought the fresh blood on Emily's arm and shoulder was hers. It only took a couple of heartbeats for him to reason that the young cop from the hallway was the one who had been injured.

Noah cast off the sling so he could better assist two nurses who had stepped up to tend to Anderson, and when he next looked for Emily, she was gone. His heart leaped and so did he, bursting into the hallway. An elevator door was just closing. He caught a glimpse of a police uniform.

The stairway was faster than waiting for another elevator, so he ran down two flights and reached the lobby just as the doors of the elevator in question were sliding open. There were two Paradise police officers on board. Neither of them was Emily Zwalt.

His head swiveled, his nerves jumping and his pulse a runaway train. "Did you see her?" he shouted at the cops. "Emily Zwalt. Did you see her?"

Instead of responding as Noah had expected, the officers separated, approaching on either side of him. One had his hand on his holster while the other began to speak. "Easy buddy. Simmer down and tell us what happened."

Incredulous, Noah raised both hands in front of him—and realized they were bloody. No one had to tell him what was about to happen. Nevertheless, he tried to explain.

"I didn't hurt anybody. I swear. A suspect did something to the officer on duty on three." Names whirled through his mind. "Anderson. Steve Anderson. That was his name."

One of the burly officers was close enough to grab Noah's wrist. He didn't resist.

"I'm telling you. Emily Zwalt took off after the assailant. We have to find her. She could be in trouble." *And she's having trouble walking, let alone running,* Noah added to himself. That would have slowed her down, especially if she'd taken the stairs.

As they turned him to cuff both wrists behind his back, Noah realized the pain in his arm had returned. He winced. "Easy, okay? See the bandage?"

One of the officers was on his radio. The other kept hold of Noah's good arm, listening to his partner's conversation.

Everyone heard a shout echo through the otherwise quiet lobby. "No! Not him."

Noah's senses absorbed Emily's presence before registering her words. She was safe! That was all that mattered. "Thank you, God."

She was at his side in seconds. "Let him go. He's with me."

The other officers were slow to comply, probably because she was once again sporting a stained uniform, although this time, Noah noted, it wasn't nearly as bad as before.

Emily was flushed and out of breath. "Let him go.

Did either of you see a woman in a long white doctor's coat?"

"She wasn't on the elevator by surgery," Noah volunteered. "I saw these guys and thought it was you, so I ran down."

She pointed. "That stairway?"

"No." He shook his head. "The one on the other end. Over there."

"Then we've covered them both," Emily said, nodding and apparently considering alternatives.

"She might have gone up instead of down," Noah offered. He was holding his hands away from his body, wishing he could wash, when he noticed Emily looking at her own share of poor Anderson's blood.

"Okay, here's what we'll do," Emily said with authority. "The hospital is locked down, so if she's still in here, she can't get out. We need to clean up and join the search since we're the only ones who know exactly what she looks like." She turned to the other two PPD officers. "See that the word is passed to all floors. Female, medium height, approximately a hundred thirty pounds, dark, stringy hair, worn jeans and dirty white shoes. She's probably shed the doctor's coat by now."

"What about Laura's husband?" Noah asked.

"That description is already being circulated. Maybe we can kill two birds with one stone."

Noah arched an eyebrow. Emily shook her head. "I'll rephrase that. Maybe we can catch two perps with one search party. How's that?"

He had to smile despite the difficult situation. "Better." As the others walked away to join newly arriving officers, Noah eyed her clothing. "You need another fresh uniform."

"I'll work on this one with a little peroxide. Catching the woman who caused it comes first."

"You'll be all right if I just duck in over there and wash?" He gestured toward a restroom sign.

The smile she gave him felt both warm and cynical. "I'm the one with the gun, remember? I'm safe."

Feeling his cheeks heating, he turned away. It was hard to keep from feeling protective toward her, no matter how well armed she was. That was ridiculous, of course. It was also an apparently ingrained reaction, because it kept popping up.

As Noah shouldered open the swinging door to the main floor restroom, he looked back at Emily. She, too, was moving toward a place to clean up. Instinct made Noah want to call out to her, to stop her from getting out of his sight.

Sensibility and a touch of embarrassment stopped him. She was right. She was perfectly capable of taking care of herself. He didn't have to shadow her everywhere she went. That was not only foolish, it was unnecessary, and he knew it. He really did.

A shiver shot up his spine as she passed out of his sight. One thing was certain. Now that he'd gotten to know her again, he was never going to stop worrying about her. The only saving grace was the fact that once Max got well, he could go back to a big-city job and forget this brief interlude in Paradise. Hopefully, he'd then be able to put Emily Zwalt out of his thoughts. How anybody could stand being part of the stressful daily life of a cop was beyond him.

Standing at the sink, soaping his hands, Noah looked at himself in the mirror and sighed. He'd thought he was in love more than once, and the idea that any of those women would *choose* to live in peril all the time was unthinkable.

That Emily did so was so unacceptable, it caused him actual physical pain.

Most of the blood was on her forearm and one shoulder, so Emily concentrated on those areas, managing to get herself clean enough for the present. She had one more change of uniform stored at the station, but that was the least of her concerns at the moment.

As she scrubbed and blotted with paper towels, she muttered to herself, "A woman attacker. Twice now." There was no doubt this time, and the hand that had been holding the knife could definitely belong to the assailant they had faced there in the hospital. Was it the same woman? Maybe. Probably. Time would tell. If prints lifted from her bedroom matched ones in the recovery room, it would do a lot to ID the assailant.

"If they know to look," she added, reaching for her radio and keying the mic. "This is Zwalt. Whoever hurt Anderson may have left fingerprints on medical equipment near the Bright woman's bed."

Affirmative replies overlapped each other. "And tell the chief I'm in the lobby. I'll be back up to the third floor ASAP."

It was Rowlings himself who answered. "Copy. Where's that lawyer you had with you?"

"He's down here, too."

"You have eyes on him?"

"I did when all this went down," Emily replied. "He's in the men's room, washing up. He's not involved other than that the Bright woman is his client."

Rowlings paused and cleared his throat. "I'm not

convinced," the chief said flatly. "Don't turn your back on him."

She wanted to reassure her boss but refrained. There was no way Noah Holden could be responsible for this crime spree, yet he might be unknowingly involved. Anything was possible, given his profession and the history he had with the serial killer's victims.

For the first time since she'd seen him again, Emily began to wonder if there was a connection to Noah that encompassed everything. Suspecting that was stretching a point, she knew, and yet…

She dried her clean hands, used the damp paper towels to wipe dry the sink area where she'd splashed water, then balled up the towels to throw them away.

Upon entering the restroom, she'd checked to make sure she was alone before relaxing enough to wash. Now, she felt a shiver shooting up her spine. That was ridiculous, of course. Nobody else had entered after her, and the place had been deserted before. There was no reason for uneasiness.

"So what's wrong with me?" she asked herself, looking around for threats.

A sudden urge to return to Noah and make sure he wasn't in danger came over her. Hurrying to the door, she pulled it open. A member of the hospital maintenance staff had placed a portable yellow-and-orange caution sign on the floor just outside and was waiting to push her cleaning cart through the door.

A mop and brooms partially obscured the woman's face, and Emily was so intent on reaching Noah, she dropped her guard for a split second. "Sorry. Excuse me." She started to sidle past.

The cart slammed into her side, driving her body into the door jamb. Her injured knee buckled. She tried to reach her gun and found it pinned behind the edge of the metal door frame.

Someone screeched. Running footsteps mingled with shouting in a cacophony of sound.

As the pressure of the metal cleaning cart eased, Emily was able to reach her sidearm and draw it. The scene was a montage of dark police uniforms and hospital scrub outfits in green and blue. Everyone blurred together, so Emily kept her gun pointed toward the ceiling.

"Get her!" a man shouted. *Noah!* That was Noah.

Emily tried to sort out the crowd, focused on his face, and felt a jolt of relief. "Where is she?"

Following the line of his gaze and the way he was pointing, she gasped. The guards who had been watching the nearest exit had left their posts to come to her aid. Nurses and hospital employees had gathered around her—all except one.

A slim figure wearing soiled white shoes had pressed a handicap release for the automatic doors and was hurrying out of the hospital.

Emily grabbed her radio and broadcast. "All units in and around the Paradise hospital. Suspect escaping wearing green scrubs and dirty shoes. East door."

Breathing was painful enough to keep her from giving chase herself. She holstered her gun and clasped that hand hard to her side, angry at herself as well as at her attacker. Whoever this was, the woman was taking her out of the fight one injury at a time, and Emily was *not* happy.

She was also not about to give up.

Noah tried to support Emily with an arm around her, but she shoved him away. Judging by the way she'd winced at his touch, her unwelcome reaction was more about pain than personal rejection.

"Are you hurt?"

"No," she snapped, grimacing.

He knew better. She was hurt all right. Not enough to slow her down the way her sore knee had, but she was in pain nonetheless.

Despite his misgivings, Noah gave ground. "Okay. What now?"

"Beats me."

Following at a short distance, he boarded the elevator with Emily and several other cops, remaining silent to keep from calling attention to himself. As long as they overlooked his presence, he'd be allowed to stay close. Nothing else mattered to him, at least for the present. Too many elements were unknown for anyone to relax, especially somebody like him who was outside the loop of vital information. The more he could pick up by listening to official sources, the better.

Chief Rowlings was waiting for his officers on the surgery floor and led them into an unoccupied room. Noah knew he'd been spotted when the chief gestured at him. "Close the door behind you, Holden."

The command had been ambiguous enough that Noah chose to interpret it to his advantage and closed himself inside with the police instead of staying out in the hall. Although Rowlings did raise a bushy, graying eyebrow, he let Noah stay.

"All right, here's what we know for sure," the chief began.

Listening, Noah was watching Emily instead of her boss. She was moving a little stiffly but seemed otherwise uninjured. Judging by the way the edge of that heavy cart had hit her—and the way she'd jumped away from his light touch—she could be nursing bruised ribs. Not that she'd admit to anything that would put her out of commission when there was a dangerous escaped attacker, maybe a murderer, to pursue.

The chief mentioned Emily's home, capturing Noah's full attention.

"The prints on the window frame at Zwalt's look like a match for what we just lifted from the recovery room, and we're processing the cleaning cart in-house, although it appears the perp wore gloves when she handled that."

Noah saw Emily nodding and was pleased to hear her ask, "Since she was after Ms. Bright, have we cleared the husband?"

Rowlings said, "Yes. Jim Bright has been exonerated by his wife's testimony. He may be a lousy husband, but he apparently didn't stab her."

"What about a possible link to the other blonde women? Anything there?"

"Not that we can tell," the chief said. "I've decided to request FBI assistance. They aren't ready to send a team yet but are standing by. Time will tell."

Noah hoped he didn't flinch when someone else asked about the body he'd found in the park.

"So far, there's no evidentiary connection," Rowlings said. "That's one thing the FBI is doing for us. I've sent them all our evidence in the hopes they can uncover some clues we've missed." At that point, his gaze sought out Noah and stayed.

Raising both hands, palms toward the group, Noah shook his head. "I'm not a bit worried. I told you I rolled her over to see if she needed first aid. I trust the evidence to prove I'm innocent of anything else."

Although there was a murmured undertone of dissension from the others, Noah felt well prepared to refute any suggestion of his closer involvement.

His fondest hope was that Emily would believe in him regardless. Choosing to avoid analyzing that desire didn't alter the truth. Her opinion mattered more than that of anyone else. And that was scary.

TEN

What Emily had yearned to do was hop into the first available patrol car and pursue her escaping suspect as far and as fast as necessary to apprehend her. She wanted to fix her mistakes and redeem the good reputation she'd earned in the Paradise Police Department. Unfortunately, her chief didn't give her that option.

"I don't need leave time. I can recuperate on the job," she argued.

Rowlings was not swayed. "If you'd been at the top of your game when these latest attacks came, you'd have handled things differently. I want you to take the rest of this week off, then get a doctor's release before reporting in on Monday."

The aching in her head was so bad she could almost take her pulse in her throbbing temples, which was why Emily didn't continue to object. So far, she had a lump on her head, an injured knee and now sore ribs. And her sidekick, whether she wanted him to be there or not, was nursing a cut on his upper arm. Even acting together, they lacked the motor skills of one able-bodied cop.

She scrunched up her face and directed it at Noah. "Don't look so pleased."

"I'm only happy because I was worried about you," he said flatly. "You may be a great cop, but..."

"What do you mean, '*may* be'?"

"Okay, okay. You *are* a great cop, but you still need to be in top form to do your job."

"My brain works just fine."

Rowlings cut in. "Good. Then pull up the files on your laptop and spend your time off figuring out what has been going on. That should keep you occupied."

"And out of trouble. I get it." Emily almost gasped when the chief followed up with, "And you, Holden, work with her and fill in the blanks. There has to be more you're not telling us."

Noah held up his hands as if his arm had already healed, although she did see a small spot of red on his bandage. Truth to tell, it would be better if both of them rested and healed before anything else drew them deeper into this puzzle.

"I promise you, Chief, I've been totally honest about those women. I barely knew them. Not like I know..." He broke off, but Emily got the idea. Even though they had never been romantically involved, they did know each other pretty well on a platonic level, not that she'd been the one to keep it that way when she was an impressionable teen.

Sighing, she pictured Noah as the young man she'd once admired. Not knowing how difficult his home life had been, she'd mistakenly assumed he had kept her at arm's length for other reasons. Her childhood had been a picnic compared to his, hadn't it? And later? Later, she'd decided that handsome cop Jake Barnes would make a perfect husband and had accepted his engagement ring. That was right before her life had nose-dived into a pit of despair, thanks to a judge and a defense attorney, she added silently.

A light touch on her elbow startled Emily and drew her mind back into the present. Everyone seemed to be looking at her as if waiting for her answer to a question she hadn't registered hearing. "Sorry, what?"

Noah half smiled. "I figured you hadn't heard what your boss said because you took it too calmly." The smile grew. "He wants us to set up a visual record of any crimes even remotely connected to what's been happening."

Confused, Emily frowned. "We have a murder board at the station."

"At your house," Noah explained, "so we can study it while recovering from our assorted injuries."

"Bad idea. Bad, bad idea," Emily snapped back. "I won't be able to rest if I'm looking at the cases all the time."

It did not please her to hear both Noah and her chief chuckling. Folding her arms across her chest, she stared at both men. "What's so funny?"

"You are," Noah said. "There is no way a busy brain like yours is going to be able to let this go, even without reminders. Putting up the board will help you focus, and maybe it'll even give my memory a boost. We won't know until we try, will we?"

"We?" Her eyebrows arched, head tilting quizzically at Noah for a few seconds before she turned to the chief. "I really don't think this is a very good idea. After all, a lot of these latest problems occurred when we were together."

"Proving that Holden here wasn't the cause," Rowlings said. "Tell you what. Instead of going home to your house or to his apartment, why don't you both move into a safe house on the outskirts of Springfield? It's only a few miles out of your way."

Emily immediately opened her mouth to protest and was stopped by the chief. "Don't go getting riled up. I didn't mean for you to break any moral codes. There's a stakeout taking place off Battlefield, and I'm rotating two teams in and out for surveillance, so you won't be there alone. Plus, that will give you backup if any of your unidentified enemies manage to track you down."

"As long as I can come and go for work if I have to," Noah said. "I won't feel comfortable locked in."

Yeah, no kidding. "Strictly voluntary?" Emily asked, making sure.

"Absolutely. Our people won't mind, and I can quit waiting for one or both of you to get attacked again."

She felt Noah's steady gaze and shivered. "I suppose we can give it a try for a short time, as long as we're free to move around as needed. I'll need to go home to pack a few things."

"Just civilian clothes. You won't need a uniform because you'll be officially off duty," Rowlings said. "I'll have someone see that they're taken care of." He turned to Noah. "What about you? What will you need?"

"Laptop, paper files. I won't know which clients until I check with my office. And the cell phone you took. My whole life is on it."

"Ah, sorry. It's in the hands of the FBI, I'm afraid."

"I want it back. Soon," Noah said firmly. "They can pair it with another phone and transfer everything over. I need that information in order to do my job properly." His jaw clenched, his eyes narrowing. "Understood?"

Rowlings was nodding. "Simmer down. I'll have it for you by tomorrow at the latest. I promise."

It wouldn't have surprised Emily to hear Noah say

something negative at that point, but his self-restraint held. Given similar circumstances, she wasn't sure she'd have been so silent. After all, there wasn't the slightest bit of evidence tying Noah to the actual crimes, and the chief was pushing it by including him in the pool of possible suspects.

Part of the problem, she realized, was that they were astonishingly short of persons of interest regarding the murder spree. It was assumed that because the victims were all young, pretty women of a certain description, the perpetrator was male.

As much as Emily hated to admit it, her chief's suggestion made sense. Seeing images and info posted should give her a better overall view of everything that had been going on.

She shivered. It was one thing to search for a person or persons who had harmed someone else. It was quite another to be hunting a predator whose intended prey was yourself.

Noah decided to personally visit Max one more time before leaving the hospital. Keeping the older man informed was necessary for Max's well-being, of course, but there was more to it now. If anything happened to Noah, Max might have to hire someone else to fill in until he was well enough to return to work himself.

Max's personal assistant, Olivia Brooks, was holding his hand when Noah knocked, then peeked in. "Sorry to bother you, but there have been some developments you should know about." He noted the tug Olivia gave to pull away and that Max kept hold of her hand, so he smiled and added, "Sorry to interrupt."

Max smiled too. "It's no secret, son. Olivia and I have known each other for years. Been friends. Worked together. But it took my stroke to wake us up to other possibilities for our future." As he spoke, his eyes glistened, and he gazed fondly at the middle-aged widow at his bedside.

Although Noah was a little taken aback, he returned Max's grin. "Good for you."

"Good for both of us," Max said. "When I thought of retiring and realized Olivia wouldn't be a part of my life anymore if I did, I decided to pay more attention to my feelings for her." He paused, apparently gathering his thoughts, then chuckled. "I almost had another stroke when she said she felt the same about me."

A sense of loss washed over Noah, as if seeing Max and Olivia happy had somehow accentuated his own separateness. He'd often assured himself that a life partner would someday cross his path, but the older he got, the more unlikely that seemed. Perhaps a deep friendship like Max and Olivia shared was what had been missing in his prior relationships. There just never seemed to be time to develop anything akin to what they'd found.

And whose fault was that? Noah asked himself. Truth to tell, he had no idea. Nor did he know what a good marriage looked like. Oh, he had plenty of examples via his adult friends, but no real inside information, no concrete assurance that he could make a go of being a husband and father. If he was honest with himself, he'd have to admit that that was the underlying problem. He'd rather stay single than create the kind of unhappy family he'd been part of growing up. If Max hadn't befriended him as a youth and kept him on the track to college, no telling what might have become of him.

Grateful beyond words, Noah shook Max's hand

and placed a brotherly kiss on Olivia's blushing cheek. "Congratulations."

They both thanked him as he straightened and backed away from the bed. "I'm glad I stopped in to hear the good news, but I have other information for you." Driving one fist into his opposite palm, he ignored the twinge in his arm. "I'm going to have to go into temporary seclusion with the police so they can pick my brain about the murders I told you about."

"You're not a suspect," Max said, frowning.

"No, no. It's not that. There was another incident today that involved a client who resembles the prior victims, and they want to immerse me in a case study in the hopes something will come to me that helps their investigation."

"What do you think?" Max asked.

"I think they're stretching. They're desperate, and there's a local officer who needs R and R, so we're going to spend some time together, talking it through, for as long as it takes."

Because Max didn't seem perturbed, Noah went on. "I'm supposed to get my phone back ASAP and will be free to drop in at the office if necessary, but I'll be basically secluded, working with the police."

"Sounds like a good basis for future work here in Paradise," Olivia interjected. She smiled. "If you decide to stay, that is."

Noah didn't comment. The last thing he wanted to do was upset his mentor, and as things stood, it might be weeks or even months before the older man would be ready to return to work. He'd already told Max he didn't feel at home in Paradise. That was enough for now.

"I'll get you other numbers to call if you need me before they return my cell," Noah said.

Max was nodding slowly. "I'd also appreciate any interesting notes you generate while they're picking your brain. Who knows? I—we—might see something you've overlooked."

"That you might," Noah agreed. "I seem to be a couple moves behind whenever this perp surfaces. The latest attack that may be connected occurred this morning. Fortunately, this victim is going to survive." He chose to not go into too much detail until the police gave him permission. "I'll email you copies of the official reports and anything else I think is pertinent." Noah looked to Olivia. "Shall I send them to the office computer or a personal one?"

"I'm doing my best to keep Max in the loop," she said sweetly. "You can email it all to me, and I'll sort it out for him."

Max reached for her hand again and clasped it. "She's kept me on the right track for twenty years."

"And will for another twenty, at least," Noah said in parting. "I should report back to Chief Rowlings."

"Who's he sending with you?" Max asked.

The pleased expression on the older man's face hinted that he already knew. Noah told him anyway. "Officer Zwalt."

"Ah, little Emily. Splendid."

Noah rolled his eyes. "*Little Emily* is one tough, determined cop. She's not at all the sweet kid I remembered. She's changed. A lot."

"I saw that when she was here with you. Still, there's a core of the person she used to be before that tragic loss."

"Jake, you mean."

"She told you?"

"Briefly. She said they were engaged when he died, and that's why she became a cop. In his memory, I guess."

Sobering, Max blinked back tears and stared out the window, unseeing. He sighed. "Jake was a good man, but..."

"Don't tell me anything negative about him, okay? I don't want to have to keep it from Emily."

"Wise," Max said. "Very wise. I look forward to hearing what you two manage to piece together. I have high hopes."

"Don't get too confident," Noah said with a tilt of his head and a farewell wave. "We haven't made much progress so far."

He was almost out the door when he heard chuckling and turned. Olivia was blushing, too.

"What?"

"Sorry," she replied, "it was just the way you said you haven't made much progress with Emily. Max and I disagreed."

She waved him off, and Noah let the door close behind him. He supposed it was natural for bystanders to assume he had a personal interest in Emily, given the time they'd recently spent in each other's company, but this was just business, that's all.

The mere thought that they were developing a fresh closeness, a special friendship, was unacceptable. The woman was crazy-brave and far too independent to suit him. The more he allowed himself to have feelings for her, the worse he worried about her safety, now and in the future. It was already going to be torture to leave Paradise, knowing she willingly faced danger daily.

Of course Max saw things differently because his faith sustained him. So did Noah's, except he believed that God expected His children to use common sense or He wouldn't have given it to them in the first place.

So, what was the sensible thing to do in this instance?

Noah asked himself. A smart man would walk away from all this, refuse to be sequestered, go straight back to work without delay and let the cops handle their own problems. Right?

What was he going to do? His unspoken answer made him smile and shake his head as he boarded the elevator and pushed the button for the third floor.

He had no choice. He was going back for Emily.

ELEVEN

The safe house was nondescript and blended into the semi-seedy neighborhood perfectly. Paint was peeling on the eaves, the lawn was sparse, and dead or dying plants abutted the foundation. Coverings for the windows looked suitably faded all right, but on closer inspection, Emily realized it was impossible to actually peer into the house past the tattered drapery because there was an additional masking layer inside.

As she piloted her unmarked car up the driveway and around to the rear, a garage door rose so she could pull directly in. The door closed behind them. She smiled at Noah. "Well, well. State of the art."

"I'm impressed," he said. "What do we do now, sneak into the house through a secret tunnel?"

"I think we just walk in," Emily joked back. "Can't have everything. Come on."

A slightly paunchy, middle-aged man greeted them at the back door with, "Welcome to my humble home," and a slight bow from the waist. Emily knew he had to be law enforcement, but he sure didn't look like it.

She extended her hand. "Pleased to meet you, Mr...."

"Smith will do. Jones is sleeping. We go on duty soon."

"This is Noah Holden," Emily said. "I'm Officer Zwalt. Emily."

Smith shook her hand, then Noah's. "We do our best to dress and act like normal citizens while we're here. No titles, no real names, you know the drill."

"Gotcha," Emily said. "They told us we could clean up and get a change of clothes here until our own stuff is delivered."

"Sure thing," Smith said, eyeing Noah's expensive shoes, shirt and slacks. "I recommend you stick to the sweat suits and worn jeans we have in your size and ditch the custom-tailored stuff. You look far too prosperous."

"I need to dress better than this when I'm arguing a case," Noah countered. "I'll play along for now, but I'm going to need a good suit and a couple of my own shirts for when I go to work."

Emily caught the older man's eye and nodded so slightly she was sure Noah wouldn't notice. He surprised her by frowning and tilting his head to the side.

"You aren't a prisoner," she told him. "But you have to admit, every time you come and go, you're opening us to discovery and possible attack."

"Opening *you*, you mean." He gently flexed his arm. "I was just in the wrong place at the wrong time."

"More than once," she countered, hoping to distract him by talking to Smith. "So, point him to his room and me to mine. Our belongings should be delivered soon."

"The chief is having some other stuff sent over, too. Where will you want to set up?"

"All the windows are blacked out?"

Smith was nodding.

"Okay." Leading the way into a rectangular dining room she'd seen from the entry, she swept an arm over the table. "We'll need this and the narrow end of the room to set up our whiteboard. Will that work for the rest of you? I don't want to be in the way."

"We just sleep and eat here," he said. "The whole place is basically yours." He pointed to Noah. "And his. Knock yourselves out. Just don't go slamming doors or playing the radio too loud. The guys coming off shift need their beauty sleep."

"Gotcha." Emily chose the empty bedroom closest to the front of the house. By the time Noah changed and rejoined her, she was dressed in pink sweats and hard at work assembling her makeshift squad room. A lanky man in his thirties who looked like he could use a good meal or two was shoveling in cereal from a large bowl and watching her. He nodded to Noah.

Spotting Noah instantly lifted Emily's mood. "Hi. Room okay?"

"Fine. I don't mind sharing."

"I beg your pardon?"

Eyes twinkling, Noah said, "You should. You get a room all to yourself, and I have to bunk in with the guy who snores."

"How do you know? Isn't he still out on assignment?"

"Doesn't matter," Noah teased. "He was the only one nobody wanted to sleep near, so he has to be a snorer."

"What happened to 'innocent until proven guilty'?"

"Some things are easy to figure out, that's all." He rounded the table and took a closer look at the photos already printed and posted.

"I hope this effort turns out to be the same," Emily said. "I'm almost done."

Noah didn't comment, so she studied his expression. His concentration was intense, his brow knitting. She had grouped the crime scene pictures below those of the victims in happier times. Several were crowd shots that included more than one of them.

As Emily tacked up the last print, Noah pointed. "There."

"What is it? What do you see?"

She noted his color paling as he continued to study a scene shot. "Behind Kit," he said. "See?"

Emily had to lean in close to see what he was trying to show her. The image was blurry, and prior to seeing Noah again, she might have failed to recognize his more mature image, but it was him all right. Him and the waitress and Annie Hackett, the killer's second victim. Noah had his arm around the pretty blonde's shoulder while Kit Lovell served them.

"Can you make it any larger?" Noah asked quietly. "I'd like a better look."

"I have the original scanned into my laptop. Give me a minute, and I'll pull it up for you."

When he said, "Thanks," Emily was positive he was anything but thankful, and her heart went out to him. Losing Jake had nearly destroyed her, and she hadn't been directly responsible. If Noah learned he was somehow the catalyst for the deaths of these young women, it was bound to leave a scar, whether he still felt close to them or not.

Yes, she wanted to solve this case. No, she didn't want to cause her old friend pain as a result, but if that was inevitable, then so be it. People had died. It was her job to pick Noah's memory enough to figure out what was causing a killer to continue taking lives.

So far, it looked as though he was the only thing connecting every victim, including Laura Bright.

Noah sat at the dining room table, staring at the computer screen and examining the photo file Emily had provided. It was eerie seeing this part of his past captured in such detail. Considering how much video was taken every second of every day and night, it was unimaginable to think that anybody got away with criminal acts.

Curious about the sources of the pictures, he asked Emily where they had come from.

"We asked friends of the victims for any records they had of the deceased from as far back as their acquaintance went. Most were from college days." She circled to show him, laying her hand over the computer mouse.

"Wait. Stop." Noah reached for the mouse and found his fingers resting atop Emily's. Because she didn't jerk away, he left his hand in place. Her skin was warm and soft. Her hair was damp from a shower and smelled like oranges. He looked up at her as she leaned over his shoulder. The temptation to tilt his head toward her until they touched was strong and growing stronger.

Emily turned toward him slowly. He could feel her breath on his cheek, see her lips parting slightly. Close enough to kiss. Close enough to get him in a pile of trouble if he stepped over the line, Noah reminded himself as he forced his mind back to the images on the screen, cleared his throat, and asked, "Have you been studying the backgrounds?"

"I assume an investigative team did. Why?"

He pointed. "Look at this one."

"I see a crowded dance floor. Who or what am I supposed to be looking for?"

"Me. There. See?"

When she leaned closer to look, he sat back in his chair to give her space. What he'd seen was not unusual, but it had brought back bits of buried memory.

"What about it?" Emily asked.

"I'm not sure. That picture gave me a nervous feeling and I don't know why. I wonder if something happened, either that night or in that same place."

To his surprise, Emily grinned. "Scoot over. We captured that as a screenshot. I may have the whole video."

Standing, he relinquished the chair and let her work. He'd never particularly enjoyed dancing, but his friends had often cajoled enough to get him up and moving. As far as Noah was concerned, a good long run was far superior to hopping around in time with music. Running unwound his nerves and provided a peaceful time for introspection. Some of his best, clearest thinking came about when his feet hit the ground with a steady rhythm and the rising sun gave him a sense of a new day bringing fresh opportunities.

The busier his life got, the less frequently he ran, which was actually self-defeating, he reminded himself. The trouble with jogging in and around Paradise, however, was being stopped by people who wanted to chat or relay gossip. Perhaps, now that he was incognito, he'd be able to squeeze in a little exercise in a neighborhood where he wasn't known. It was worth considering, providing he didn't get mugged. Smith was right about blending in. The less attention he called to himself, the less chance of a problem.

Emily disturbed his short reverie. "Got it!" She was pointing at the screen. "This is it, right?"

Noah peered at the grainy footage. "Looks like it. I see myself and recognize a couple of others. A few more seem familiar, but I can't think of their names." He caught himself frowning. "Sorry."

"It'll come to you. Give yourself a chance."

As he straightened, he shook his head. "That would

be fine if somebody wasn't eliminating people from my past."

"And from your present," Emily added. "Remember Laura Bright."

"How can I forget? Has there been any word on the woman who knifed Anderson at the hospital and slammed you with the cleaning cart?"

"Unfortunately, no. Partial prints on the IV by Laura's bed are a match to ones found on the jimmied window of my bedroom, but that's really all we have. There's no record of that person in any data bank."

"Too bad."

"Yeah, no kidding." Emily hesitated. "Look, why don't you stay and watch the whole video while I finish posting clues and mark possible connections between each victim. Maybe something else will occur to you if you try to imagine yourself back a few years, dancing with pretty girls."

Noah snorted a wry chuckle. "Pretty on the outside, maybe, but not always sweet inside."

"Jot that down, too," she suggested. "When a name pops into your head, make a note of it and of anything else you can recall about that person."

"It's going to be random," Noah warned her.

"That's what we want. Anything and everything. We can sort it out later. If you stop to think about each memory, your subconscious is liable to form a story. What you need to be cautious about is the mind's tendency to fill in details that aren't accurate. Our brains crave order. We want to make sense of things, and if the actual details are lacking, it's possible false ones will fill the void."

"Which is why ten people can see the same crime committed and give different descriptions."

"Right." She laid a hand gently on his forearm and looked up into his eyes. "I trust you to be totally honest with me. I just don't want you to embellish anything because you want so badly to help. Understand?"

"Completely." Noah sighed deeply. "The only reason I'm here at all is to help you, you know."

"I was afraid you were feeling responsible."

"Not at all. I've racked my brain, and I know I haven't said or done a single thing to trigger violence. Not in the past, not lately."

"How can you be sure?"

"Because my life is not lived on the edge the way yours is, Em. I don't pursue people and put them in jail. I defend them, and a big portion of my work is pro bono, as well."

He saw her gaze narrow, felt her lift her hand from his arm, saw her backing away. Finally she stood very still, looking at him as if he had just morphed into Public Enemy Number One.

"In other words," she said, "you're the good guy and I'm the villain?"

"I didn't mean that. Don't be so touchy."

"Touchy? *Touchy?* I'm a cop, Noah, and a good one. We uphold laws that most people look for ways to circumvent. And when we do catch them, society does its best to get them a slap on the wrist and send them out to continue breaking laws."

"By *society*, I take it you mean attorneys and judges."

"I do."

Hesitating to carefully choose his words, Noah decided to speak his mind. Emily certainly had. "You realize what you're doing, don't you?"

"Telling the truth," she answered quickly.

"No. You're prejudging my profession the same way

you complain that people prejudge you. Even the men and women who backed the release of the man who killed your fiancé were doing what they thought was right. All any conscientious judge or jury can do is their very best at that moment in their lives."

The sight of moisture glistening in her eyes was almost enough to stop him, but not quite. Emily was never going to heal until she was able to forgive others for what happened in the past and learn to forgive him for wanting to aid the hopeless.

Approaching, he tenderly took her hand, clasping it between both of his. "The past is the past. Yes, it hurts. It probably always will. The people involved made mistakes. Very human mistakes. We're all fallible, Emily. Even you."

She jerked her hand from his, wheeled and limped from the room, leaving Noah behind. The off-duty, cereal-eating cop made a sound of derision. "That went well." He picked up his empty bowl and gestured with it. "Next time, do what I did with this stuff."

Noah snorted. "What's that?"

"Put a little sugar on it when you try to feed it to her. A hard truth is always easier to swallow if it's sweetened."

TWELVE

A tiny spark of truth in what Noah had said kindled a bonfire in Emily's mind. She wanted to scream at him for being wrong, for not trying to understand how she felt, yet some inner force was holding her back. That was why she'd left him so abruptly and why she was presently pacing the floor in the tiny, dimly lit bedroom.

Most of the time, when criticism came her way, Emily was able to disregard it, so why did it hurt so much when Noah failed to appreciate her point of view? Surely, it wasn't because she cared more about his opinion than that of others, was it? That possibility did exist despite her best efforts to dismiss it. To dismiss *him*. Was there that much hero worship lurking in her buried memories of the young man he'd once been?

An alternative idea was whirling through her mind, and no matter how much she denied it, touches of rationality clung to the notion. Did she admire the man he had become? Was it possible to disagree so vehemently and still appreciate the good he was trying to do in the world?

"No," Emily insisted aloud in the empty room. People like Noah did their best to thwart all the good she and her fellow officers were also trying to do. How could she look up to someone who pitted himself against her?

However, he did seem to be trying to help in this instance, didn't he? Could he have touched on a glimmer of truth when he'd contrasted her attitude with that of private citizens who misunderstood the goal of the police force?

"No," she said flatly. "Just, no."

A knock on her door startled her. Expecting to see Noah, she jerked open the door. "What?"

It was Smith, and he was grinning. "At ease, Zwalt. I'm just the messenger."

"Sorry. What's up?"

The undercover cop hooked a thumb over his shoulder. "That lawyer in there is practically jumping up and down. He says he's found something."

"Gotcha. Thanks." Emily sidled past him and almost ran back down the hallway. The hopeful expression on Noah's face raised her spirits, too.

He stood and offered her the chair in front of the laptop. "Go back about ten minutes and watch this all the way through."

"What am I looking for?"

"Expressions. Don't watch me, watch the crowd. You'll see."

If Noah had not been fidgeting and standing so close behind her, Emily might have been able to concentrate better. As it was, she would have missed the clue he'd found if he hadn't pointed when the video reached the scene he'd mentioned.

"There. Along the wall. See her?"

Emily hit Pause. A nondescript woman in her twenties was leaning with her back against the wood paneling. Her arms were crossed as if she was barely able to control anger, and her eyes narrowed as they tracked Noah's progress across the room in the company of several blonde women.

"Who is that?" Emily asked him.

"Beats me. But she sure doesn't look happy. Am I imagining it, or is she glaring daggers at me? No pun intended."

"I don't think it's you," Emily replied. "I think she's staring at the girls you're with. Can you identify them?"

Leaning closer, Noah touched the screen. "That's Annie. And Kit is in the background. See?"

"What about the other one? It looks like you have a girl on each arm." As she spoke, Emily had to tamp down an undeniable jolt of jealousy.

"We were all just casual friends," Noah said. "I'm not positive about it, but that may be a roommate of Annie's. Her name's on the tip of my tongue, I just can't quite come up with it. It was kind of unusual."

"She's blonde, too." Emily started paging through the lists in the police file until she came to the one she sought. "Here. This may be her. Does Vangie Mead ring a bell?"

"I think that's it. Where is she these days?"

"Memphis," Emily said. "There's a chance she may remember who the grump is who was watching you."

"Are we going to Memphis?"

"No." Emily shook her head. "That's not necessary. We can contact the police there and have them interview her about this video. Anybody else?"

"Not so far. I still have hours of video to watch, so maybe I'll see something later."

Slipping to the side so Noah could resume his seat at the computer, Emily said, "Okay. I'll call my chief and get things moving." She took a couple of steps. "One other thing. I'm sorry I got upset at you. You're entitled to your opinion."

"And you're entitled to yours," he began smiling, "even if you are wrong."

The astonishment on Emily's pretty face was so comical Noah had to laugh. To his relief, she responded in kind. It had been so long since he'd heard her actually laugh, he was shocked that the sound was so warmly familiar. He might not remember the names of all the women he'd met since leaving Paradise, but the one he'd left behind was surprisingly unforgettable.

"Agree to disagree?" she asked.

"Yes." Noah offered his hand, and she accepted it, but instead of shaking the way business acquaintances would, he simply held her hand for a long moment. Her lack of resistance wasn't full acceptance, but it felt like a step in the right direction. Anything that broke down the walls she'd built around herself was bound to help her heal from the loss that had hardened her heart. That was one of his goals, he realized, accepting the notion easily. It had to happen.

He wanted to congratulate her for coming this far but held back. Nothing he said or did was guaranteed to reinforce this change in her opinion, and the less he drew attention to their newly found middle ground, the better.

"I'll get back to work, shall I?" Noah suggested, canting his head toward the computer.

"Of course. Absolutely. I'll call Chief Rowlings and explain everything. He can take it from there."

"Good." Noah picked up a pencil and jotted down the time stamp on the video he'd been watching so he could locate it again. When he looked up, Emily had her back to him and was speaking into her phone. He couldn't help overhearing.

"I'll take a couple of screenshots and forward the details to you. We got the video from her, so she should be easy for the Memphis department to locate."

Replying to whatever Rowlings said next, Emily added, "Yes. He's still working on it. Yes, you were right. He's one of the good guys."

Noah didn't care whether she ever told him the same thing or not. It was enough to hear her admit it to her boss. The funny thing was, he truly didn't care what most people thought of him as long as he was doing his God-given job to the best of his ability. Max mattered, of course. So did Olivia. But beyond them and a few men he'd worked with in the city, the only other person whose opinion carried any weight at all was Emily Zwalt. *Officer* Emily Zwalt.

That was the biggest drawback. If he'd been positive she'd entered law enforcement because of a dedication to the profession, he might not be so concerned. Unfortunately, the more he learned about her past and saw the way she behaved on duty, the more he questioned her true motives.

If, as she claimed, she had chosen to become a police officer to enforce laws and keep the peace, then fine. Since her wounded heart had led her there in order to right a wrong that could never be changed, she was liable to take too many chances and risk her own life too often.

Someday, somehow, he was going to have to try to get her to see that mending a broken heart didn't require a full-on, frontal attack. It wasn't nearly that easy. They all carried invisible scars that would always be with them. Emily had the tools to work with to effect

public, of which he was part. The job of keeping them both safe was hers. She took that vow seriously. All the cops she knew did. Their problem then became when to act and when to hold their fire. Thankfully, pulling the trigger was a choice she'd never been called upon to make.

In her heart she knew it would be a split-second decision if it happened. Her choice could mean the difference between life and death for herself and anyone else in imminent danger, and yet it was still going to be difficult to pull that trigger.

Remembering prior attacks, how Noah had been injured at her house and Officer Anderson at the hospital, she steeled herself for the possibility of having to harm one fellow human being to save another. Could she? Would she?

Picturing her late fiancé and the lethal situation in which he'd lost his life, Emily realized for the first time that she was also blaming him. He'd been shot by a known criminal, yes, but forensics had shown he'd never returned fire. He'd had time to draw his service weapon as he'd taken cover behind a nearby vehicle. He'd been in position to shoot. But he had not. A lethal bullet had passed through the car's door and ended his life. His career. And erased all her dreams for a happy future.

Unshed tears misted her vision. Growing angrier by the second, she shook off feelings of loss and frustration, replacing them with a vow to never be weak, never back down.

Taking a deep breath to embrace her resolve, Emily felt the bruises on her ribs and clamped her jaw. Mistakes might be tolerated in other professions, but they could prove deadly in hers. They already had, far too often.

With her holdout gun strapped to her ankle and service weapon tucked under the copious sweatshirt she was wearing, she threw the switch to raise the garage door and hurried to check the cruiser. The trunk held a veritable arsenal as well as flares for traffic accidents, first aid equipment, rescue breathing masks and the protective vests she'd hoped for.

Seeing Noah bolting from the house and running toward her, she thrust a vest at him. "Put this on."

"Bulletproof?" he asked.

"This is the best defense we have," Emily informed him. "Wear it under your clothes so you won't be conspicuous." He proceeded to take off his hoodie and start to don the vest over his T-shirt while she showed him the tabs on each side. "Do you have one on already?" he asked, eyeing her.

"They're all too big for me."

Freezing in midmotion, he stared. "Then I'm not wearing one, either."

"Don't be ridiculous."

"Ridiculous is making me wear one when you don't."

"Okay, okay." She pulled the final Velcro tab out of his grip and slapped it against his side. "I'll put one on over my clothes to take up the slack until I can get one that fits."

Emily tightened the tabs on her vest before moving toward the driver's door. "Get that shirt back on and get in. We need to hurry."

"Why? You never said where we're going."

"To Memphis," Emily said, shouting at him over the roar of the engine inside the garage. "Their police were too slow getting to Vangie Mead."

She dropped the transmission into Reverse and backed out with a squeal of rubber on the concrete floor.

"Dead?" Noah asked, sounding breathless.

Emily fisted the wheel and shook her head as she shifted. "No. I assume she's been sedated. Rowlings wants us there when she wakes up. He's hoping she recognizes you and that jolts her memory."

"Not all that likely," Noah replied. Forward momentum pressed him hard against the back of the seat.

"Anything is possible," Emily countered. "Even the good guys getting a break now and then."

THIRTEEN

Noah saw nothing wrong with answering truthfully when she glanced across the cruiser to ask, “Are you sleeping?”

He smiled back at her. “Praying. I figured, the way you’re driving, it was a good idea.”

“Very funny.”

“It wasn’t meant to be,” he said, tightening his grip on the handhold by the door. “Is the Mead woman going to be okay?”

“I assume so,” Emily replied. Noah saw her punching buttons on her steering wheel before she spoke aloud again. “Dispatch, this is Zwalt. En route to Memphis. Chief’s orders. Can you give me an update on the condition of the hospitalized victim?”

“Stand by.”

In seconds, the dispatcher reported, “The Memphis victim is heavily sedated. I’m patching you through to the chief.”

Emily’s eyebrows arched, and Noah noticed a tightening of her fingers on the steering wheel.

Rowlings’s voice was gruff. “Location?”

“Coming up to the cutoff to Paradise. I was going to

stop for my vest and an extra gun if you think there's time."

"The situation here has changed since we spoke. Report to the station."

"What's happened?"

"Plenty. We have another victim."

Staring at her, Noah saw Emily's eyes widen and her hands tremble slightly. "Known or unknown?"

"We have an ID," the chief said, "but she's not blonde. We'll fill you in when you get here."

"Don't you want me to go straight to the scene?"

"No."

Relief washed over Noah when Rowlings ordered her to come to the station. After all, she had yet to be cleared by a doctor to go back to work, and although she was driving as if primed for anything, he had his reservations about her readiness. It wasn't enough to be game and brave to a fault, which she was. She also needed to be in top form, for her sake as well as that of others.

Others like me, Noah thought, feeling as if he should be protecting her instead of the reverse. Actually, he was looking out for her, he amended. Sticking together was part of fulfilling his role, as was watching all those videos and racking his brain for connections beyond himself.

And now there was another victim in Paradise. Closing his eyes and turning back to silent prayer, he couldn't help hoping that this latest victim was a stranger to him.

Emily slowed once she left the highway. The streets of Paradise were mostly deserted at this predawn hour. There was activity around the police station, though, and lights blazed at the twenty-four-hour gas station.

Something about the scene bothered her, as if her subconscious had picked up a warning that her conscious mind was having trouble processing. She didn't like that feeling one bit and said so.

"Does everything look normal to you?" she asked Noah.

"As normal as ever, I guess. Why?"

"I don't know. Intuition?"

"Nothing wrong with that," he said. "Talk to me. Maybe something will come to you."

"It's not that simple," Emily argued. "Haven't you ever gotten the willies for no apparent reason?"

"Only when taking the bar exam," he said, smiling over at her. "Do you get these feelings often?"

She shook her head. "No. That's the problem. I must have seen something that set off alarm bells."

"I'm sorry," Noah said, "I wasn't really paying attention. Want to circle around and take a second look?"

"No. I don't want to keep the chief waiting."

Remaining tense, Emily wheeled into the lot behind the station and parked. Nothing looked out of order, and overhead lights blazed.

She got out and stretched.

The singing whine of a rifle bullet sliced through the darkness. Instinct kicked in. She dropped into a crouch between the chassis and car door, drew her weapon, and took up a defensive posture. Before she had time to shout to Noah to get down, the rifle fired again. This time, glass shattered.

There was a sharp cry. Men with shotguns and pistols ready poured out the rear door of the station and deployed the way a military patrol would if they came under fire.

Her radio squawked. "Zwalt?"

Emily cautiously rose up enough to reach across the driver's seat for her mic. "I'm parked behind the main station. Taking fire."

"You're not hit?"

Outside her vehicle, men were shouting to each other so she raised her voice to be heard. "No, I'm fine."

Next to her, still belted into the passenger seat, Noah made a strange noise. Emily's grip on the mic tightened so much she was broadcasting when she shouted at him. "Noah!"

A quick assessment showed her the trajectory of the second bullet. It had shattered the rear window, pierced the top of the back seat, passed through the upright section of the passenger seat, and hit Noah in the back. His head was bowed, his eyes closed, and she couldn't be sure he was breathing.

Grabbing his wrist she felt for a pulse, and found a strong, racing beat. That was enough for instantaneous thankfulness, followed by the urge to throw her arms around him in celebration.

Instead, she undid his seat belt, pushed open the door on the far side of the car and nudged him until he looked at her. "Get out. Stay down."

Clambering over the seat after him she tried to shield him, "Are you hurt?"

"Yeah," he said, sounding breathless. "Feels like a road grader ran over me."

"Lean forward. Let me see."

Another gentle push gave her access to his back. There was clearly a hole punched in the hoodie. Heart pounding, she lifted it. No blood. *No blood!* Emily's voice faltered. "You're not bleeding. The vest saved your life."

Wide-eyed, he gaped at her. “I’m not shot? Are you sure?”

“Positive. You felt the impact, but it didn’t break the skin.”

“How about bones? I think some ribs cracked.”

In spite of his pain she was grinning at him. “Probably not. You will be sore for a while, but it beats being dead.”

“No argument there.”

The car radio broadcast, “All clear. No sign of the shooter.”

Emily rose slowly, then reached for Noah, intending to help him stand. To her surprise, he did the same, and they rose together. Moving as one, they hurried into the station while others continued to patrol outside.

He was obviously still out of breath, probably from the pain, but gamely pulled the hoodie off over his head. Velcro tabs on the protective vest made ripping sounds as Emily pulled her side loose and Noah did the other.

One more layer of clothing and she could relax, she told herself. “Turn around.”

Noah bent forward resting his hands on a desk, and she gently raised his T-shirt. A bruise was starting to form, radiating out from a red center where the bullet had nearly taken his life.

For a few seconds she stared, speechless. If she hadn’t talked him into donning the vest when she did, they could very easily be following an ambulance carrying his body to ER, or worse.

One of the other officers handed Emily a sterile alcohol wipe, and she bathed the reddening area in case there had been microscopic penetration.

Noah jumped. “Cold!”

“You should be thankful you can feel anything,”

Emily said. "Do you have any idea how close you came to…" She faltered.

"Buying the farm, as they say around here?" Noah replied. "Yes. I'm getting the idea." He cleared his throat. "Thanks for insisting I wear armor."

"You're welcome. You'll still need a comprehensive medical assessment, but in my opinion, you'll be fine."

"Until the next time," he said soberly. "You were out of the car and visible. This shooter couldn't have mistaken me for you."

A deep breath preceded her nod. "I'm afraid you may be right."

The arrival of an ambulance ended their conversation as medics shouldered through the group hovering around Noah. He caught Emily's eye. "If you aren't coming with me, I'm not going anywhere."

"Don't be silly. I'll check in with the chief and be along as soon as he's briefed me on the latest female victim."

"We're going to need a long list to keep everybody straight," Noah quipped cynically.

"Two lists, the way I see it," Emily said. "One for the blonde women and another one for you."

Rather than disagree, he chose to change the subject while one of the medics took his blood pressure. "Well, there is one good thing about what just happened."

She made a sour face. "I can hardly wait for you to tell me."

Noah gave a soft chuckle, realized it hurt and stopped. "My back has completely taken my mind off my arm. I don't even feel the stitches anymore."

With an exaggerated roll of her eyes and a loud

"Aargh!" she turned and left him to the ministrations of the paramedics.

One of them appeared at his elbow with a clipboard. "If you won't let us transport, you'll need to sign this release."

"What would they do if I went to the hospital? Same things you just did, right?"

The medic grinned. "Yup. Maybe an X-ray, too. And ice packs. You're gonna be plenty sore."

Noah grabbed the pen and signed. "Thanks guys. Appreciate it."

The medic stripped off a blue surgical glove and offered his hand to Noah. "Hang in there, man."

Shaking hands, Noah read his name on his shirt and noticed that his gaze had followed Emily across the room so he asked, "You know her, too…, Mark?"

"As much as she'll let me," Mark said.

A jolt of jealousy that hit him out of nowhere. He cleared his throat. "Emily and I go way back."

"Maybe that's your secret. I don't know."

"Maybe she already has a man in her life."

"Hah! She seems friendly enough until you try to get close to her."

Lowering his voice to speak aside, Noah said, "I heard she lost her fiancé."

"She did. I was one of the medics who worked on him. But that was years ago."

"Years?" It surprised Noah to hear that so much time had passed. "How many?"

Mark shrugged. "I don't know. Maybe five." He sighed. "It's been a while."

"I see. Not that there's a time limit on grief."

Agreeing, the medic nodded. "I think she'd have done better if she hadn't tried to do CPR on him before we got there. She was a basket case when we pronounced him."

Adding to her misplaced sense of responsibility, Noah thought. That figured. So did her transference of blame. Whether she realized it or not, she was probably angry at God, too. There were stages of grief, he knew, and it was possible to get stuck and struggle to move on. Everybody was different.

Could he help her come to grips with the loss that had apparently shaped her life for the past five years? Was he the right person to do that, considering his own lack of close human connections? If he hadn't formed a strong emotional bond with Max, he'd be a lot like Emily, wouldn't he? A loner. A person who avoided emotional involvement because he'd been burned, disappointed, had felt unworthy and unloved in the past.

Noah mentally shook off the introspection. He'd fought his way from being a neglected kid to becoming the junior partner of a respected attorney. Max had imparted more than a strong work ethic. He'd shared his faith until Noah had seen his own need for surrender and had also accepted Jesus Christ. There was little more he lacked at this point in his life. He was supremely grateful for everything.

However, he also realized that with blessings came a calling to follow where God led him. To do the right things. That was what had caused him to choose his career and what had brought him back to Paradise when he was needed.

So where did that leave him, spiritually speaking? He could see Emily across the room, deep in conversation. It wasn't that hard to imagine that he'd been sent to Paradise for her sake as well as Max's. Why not? The Maker of the Universe wasn't limited to singular reasons for things happening. Only humans had that narrow way of thinking. As he saw it, his part in this unfolding drama was to trust the Lord and do his best, just as he'd told Emily when they'd been discussing her disappointments. Beyond that, it was out of his hands. Intellect could only take a person so far.

Noah flexed his shoulders, his spine, and winced. Speaking of intellect, how were he and Emily going to find the answers to their mystery? Between them they probably had enough clues to figure it out if they just looked at the situation from a different angle or added one or two more missing facts. Deciding which events pertained to which person or persons was going to be the key.

Because criminals had habits that formed their methods, Noah was certain the string of murders had to be connected. That left the apparently random attacks on him or Emily or the police in general. When he sorted it out that way, it looked as if he was less of a target and more of a bystander who had been in the wrong place at the wrong time. It was comforting to think of himself that way. It could also be dangerous to become overly complacent.

He flexed again as he started across the room, felt the sting of the bruise the bullet had made and silently thanked God for his survival. Then he chided himself for the delay. "Better late than never."

Emily met him halfway and held up a photograph. "This is Kirsty McAdams. Tell me you don't know her."

Noah stared at the picture and sighed with genuine relief. "Never saw her before in my life."

FOURTEEN

Disappointed, Emily said, "That's too bad," before she stopped to think.

"Too bad? You *want* to tie all those poor women to me?"

"I didn't mean it that way." And she hadn't. But connections between victims would help them eventually solve these crimes, so an odd one out was an unfortunate anomaly.

It was a relief when Noah nodded and took the photo from her. "I get it. If I was the key, you'd have narrowed the list of suspects." He was staring at the smiling face in the picture. "There may be something familiar about her, but I can't recall what. It may just be because I was expecting to see someone I knew."

"Why don't you go back to the safe house and finish going through those videos?"

"Can't I do that here?"

Racking her brain for a valid excuse to deny him, she came up empty. "I suppose so, if it's okay with the chief."

She noted how he flinched when he moved too quickly. "You could just rest until you're feeling better."

"Nonsense. What's a little discomfort compared to the chance to save lives?"

There was no argument against such perfect logic. "Okay. I'll set you up in an interview room. What can I do to make you more comfortable?"

"Ice packs would be nice," Noah said. "The medics recommended that."

"Done." Emily pointed to a hallway. "Follow me."

Their footsteps were muted by the athletic shoes they both wore and let her hear her rapid heartbeats. Flashes of memory, visions of Noah collapsed in the car, kept intruding and upping her pulse rate. The urge to stop and turn, to open her arms and embrace him, grew stronger and stronger as the moments passed.

Pausing at a door at the end of the hallway, Emily looked up into his dark eyes and couldn't make herself look away. She sensed tears of thankfulness welling behind her lashes and was afraid if she blinked they'd start to trickle down her cheeks.

She willed time to stop. There was a new glistening in Noah's gaze, too. He lifted one arm, apparently intending to slip it around her shoulders. That was not going to be enough for her. Not nearly enough.

Emily stepped closer, wrapped her arms around his waist and began to give him a gentle hug.

The sensation of him returning the embrace undid her. Eyes closed, tears flowing, she laid her cheek on his chest and held on as if he was her anchor in a storm, which he was. There were no arguments left in her. No good reasons to stop what was happening so spontaneously. She needed this closeness and, if her senses weren't fooling her, Noah did, too.

At that precious moment, if she could have chosen, she would have agreed to stand there like that for the rest of her life.

A whistle split the quiet. Noah jumped away and

groaned softly. Staying behind him to block anyone from seeing, Emily quickly wiped away her tears and opened the door to the interview room. "After you, Mr. Holden."

Noah's chuckle was accompanied by a grimace but that didn't stop him. "Yes, Officer Zwalt. Whatever you say."

Leaving the door open on purpose, she stuck her head out and called to the whistler, her usual patrol partner. "Bring me my laptop, Cal. It's out in the unmarked cruiser."

"The one full of holes?" he asked, sounding amused.

"Yes. And hurry up."

Emily figured it was just as well she hadn't been able to hear his reply since he'd punctuated it with wry laughter. She gestured to Noah. "Have a seat. I'll get someone to bring you cold packs for your back."

"Emily, I'm…"

"My fault. Totally my fault," she interrupted. "Sorry. It was unprofessional of me."

"But nice," Noah said, eyeing the open door and raising an eyebrow.

"Don't go getting the wrong idea, Mr. Holden. It won't happen again. I was simply happy that you'd survived."

Noah was grinning. "I'm pretty happy about that, myself."

The arrival of Calvin Dodge with the laptop ended Emily's need for small talk and relieved some of her tension. "All right," she said, gesturing at Noah, "make yourself as comfortable as possible while I unlock this and set it up for you. Do you want to start at the beginning or pick up where you left off?"

From behind her, Dodge snorted.

"That's enough, Cal," Emily ordered. "You're excused. Go find somebody else to harass."

Although he backed toward the door, he didn't seem to be in a hurry. Without looking, Emily knew Noah had stepped closer behind her as if to provide protection, and she was not pleased.

Turning her back on Cal, she faced her erstwhile protector. "Sit down. I'm in charge here."

Noah didn't help her waning sense of control by first saluting and saying, "Yes, ma'am. Sir. Officer."

The sound of Cal's muted chuckling echoed down the hallway. In a few minutes, if it hadn't already happened, the news of her embracing Noah was going to be the talk of the station. From there, it was bound to bring amusement all over town.

Emily didn't need a mirror to tell she was blushing.

"If it's any consolation," Noah said, "I've wanted to do that for a long time."

"It isn't," she insisted, wondering if she was telling the truth or merely fooling herself. The laptop rested on the interview table in front of Noah. Emily could have moved it or turned it around and seated herself on the opposite side of the table, but she didn't.

Before she could change her mind, she rounded the table, placed a chair next to Noah's and pulled the computer to her so she could work. If he noticed a difference in her reaction he didn't mention it.

Once the correct file was opened and she'd located the right time stamp, she pushed the laptop to him. "Here you go. Have fun."

His hand reached out to touch hers. "Emily."

Pull away! her mind screamed.

Noah closed his fingers around hers. "I just want to tell you something."

"I really need to go see Chief Rowlings about the latest victim."

"In a second."

She tried to keep her gaze from meeting Noah's because she was afraid if she ever looked directly into those dark eyes of his again, she'd be trapped like before, a hapless explorer sinking in jungle quicksand. When he cupped her chin and gently raised her face to his, she was lost.

"I want you to know how blessed I am to be here with you."

Emily opened her mouth to object, but he silenced her.

"No. Let me get this out before I change my mind."

She saw him swallow hard and waited.

"Nothing about my return to Paradise was planned, yet I seem to be in the right place at the right time, and I have to believe it's no accident."

Something in Emily insisted he was right no matter how hard she tried to make herself disagree.

Noah went on. "I could have been killed several times, yet I wasn't, and since I don't believe in luck, I have to credit my Maker—and you—for my survival. I was wrong when I thought I was the only one rescuing the innocent. You're doing it too, even if you don't see past the retribution phase of your job, and I'm sorry. I misjudged you."

Embarrassed and more than a little touched, Emily eased her hand from his and sat back. "You don't need to apologize."

"Yes, I do. I'd already been thinking along those lines, and when that bullet slammed into me, I was afraid I'd lost my chance to tell you so."

Truth hit her hard. Noah was right. How many nights

had she lain awake, wishing she could reverse time and say the loving things she'd only thought about in the past?

Saying "thank you" and heading for the door because tears threatened, Emily escaped to the hallway.

Actually, she'd had a similar reaction to the one Noah had described when she'd thought he'd been shot. In a split second of intense awareness, she'd realized how deeply she cared about him. At that time, she'd entertained no criticism of his job or his motives. All that had mattered was Noah. Him. The man who seemed to be pitted against her, yet had found an empty spot in her heart to fill with appreciation of his character, his kindness and honesty, and the faith they shared.

It suddenly occurred to Emily that she was showing a lack of faith every time she lamented the loss of her late fiancé, every time anger caused her to hate lawbreakers, every time she shed a tear over the perfect future she'd dreamed of.

Sniffling, then blowing her nose in the restroom, she pulled herself together, squared her shoulders and marched back up the hall, intending to confess as much to Noah. She silently rehearsed expressions of acceptance and appreciation, words that would intelligently prove her change of heart without sounding too flowery or formal.

She had the perfect spiel ready to deliver when she opened the door to the room and peeked in. He looked up from the computer, smiled, and erased every vestige of her speech in a millisecond.

Emily's burning desire to air her feelings remained. The ideal words she'd chosen, however, did not, so she went with the first thing that popped into her head and blurted, "I'm glad you're not dead."

Noah's warm laughter followed her back down the hall and even into the chief's office until she closed the door.

There was nothing Noah wanted more than to help Emily and stop the killing. That goal kept him at the computer long past personal comfort. Finally giving in to the throbbing in his back and leaning back to stretch, he decided to refresh his concentration by taking a stroll through the station.

The Paradise facility looked small from the outside, but that was nothing compared to how tiny it was inside. Between the section set apart for cells and extra storage for supplies that were part of the police department's disaster relief program, offices took up barely half of the single-story building.

Conversation between the desks in the squad room buzzed like agitated bees in a hive—until the occupants noticed him. Then the noise damped down as if someone had flipped a switch to turn it all off at once. Judging by a few snickers and a thumbs-up gesture from Cal Dodge, Emily had been right about their embrace causing gossip. Noah wasn't sure how he felt about that, not that it mattered in the grand scheme of things. Small towns were infamous for perpetuating rumors, usually with plenty of embellishment, and his only regret was causing trouble for her.

Undeserved guilt tried to intrude on his thoughts. Noah wouldn't let it. There was nothing wrong with hugging an old friend. Nothing at all. He wasn't about to defend himself or Emily unless her boss had a problem with their newfound closeness. Even if that did happen, he had plenty of plausible excuses cataloged and ready. What he did not have, unfortunately, was new evidence to share.

He lingered near an unoccupied desk and watched her speaking to Rowlings. The chief didn't look overly impressed with whatever she was telling him, but he didn't look upset, either. That was comforting because it meant the man wasn't likely to discipline Emily for hugging a prime witness. Yes, he was innocent of any crime. Yes, he was cooperating. But as long as he wasn't coming up with any new evidence or recollections to assist the police, he figured he was being allowed to stay as a favor, period.

Racking his brain for a good reason to remain near Emily, Noah came up with one he felt was totally plausible. Now that he thought about it, there was a real possibility he could be right. There was only one way to find out.

Zigzagging between the desks, he found one that clearly reflected a feminine touch and paused there, biding his time and watching. He didn't have long to wait.

"Finished with all those tapes? Wow, I'm impressed. You're fast."

"I would be if I was done, but I'm not. I wondered, can you scare me up a print copy of the most recent victim?"

"Did you change your mind about knowing her?"

"No. It just seemed smart to see if I can spot her in the party crowd I'm watching, and I couldn't remember exactly what she looked like."

"Okay, hang on. I'll print you out a copy."

"Thanks." Noah stuffed his hands into his pants pockets and tried to appear nonchalant. "Any word on Vangie? Is she still sedated?"

"Even if she isn't, there's no real reason for us to drive all the way to Memphis to interview her."

That was disappointing. Noah shrugged. "If you say so."

"It's not up to me. If the chief thought it was necessary, he'd send us."

"I notice you keep saying *us*. Is he planning on keeping me around?" Noah asked.

"Apparently."

"I do have to spend some time at my office, you know."

Emily was nodding thoughtfully. "I know. I've been waiting for you to insist on that."

"I can stay a little longer. I checked in with Stephanie and had her move today's appointments to tomorrow. I do have one court date I can't change, but otherwise my day-to-day schedule is pretty flexible."

Assuming that would placate her, he was surprised when she frowned. "I asked the chief to assign an officer to guard you."

"And?"

"And he said we're too shorthanded."

"No problem. I can take care of myself. I always did fine before."

She fisted her hands on her hips and took a firm stance. "How many times were you shot at in the big city?"

"That's not relevant."

"Of course it is." Emily's voice was raised enough to attract attention.

"Okay. Never. But you still haven't proved to me that I'm the target."

"Humph." She sent an expression of disgust his way. "You look smarter than you sound."

Purposely changing the subject, Noah braced himself to keep from showing pain and held out his hand. "Give me that photo you promised and I'll go back to the videos."

"Pizza?" Emily asked.

"I beg your pardon."

"You have to eat, and so do I. What kind of pizza do you like? My treat."

He could tell she was trying to not smile, and as she slowly failed, he grinned back at her. "Do you mean to tell me you forgot in ten short years?"

The blush on her fair cheeks answered his question. She did remember, but he chose to lessen the pressure on her. They needed to start over. He could see now that trying to build on the amiable relationship they'd once shared wasn't going to work under current circumstances.

"No mushrooms," he said, continuing to smile. To his relief, Emily turned back to her desk and proceeded to sort paperwork that he suspected had been fine in the first place.

Watching her, really watching her, Noah realized how precious to him she was. When she wasn't acting the part of a tough, no-nonsense cop with a chip on her shoulder, she was a pretty woman. Maybe even beautiful in her own, natural way. She didn't need makeup or anything fake to be so appealing he could hardly make himself leave her.

But he had to, didn't he? Their present closeness had been brought about by outside forces. In order to see if there could be anything more between them, he had to see this confusion through to its climax, figure out the puzzle and bide his time until Emily was free to consider him a friend instead of tying him to horrible crimes.

And then what? Noah chuckled under his breath. He had absolutely no idea. All he knew for sure was that a killer or killers were out there somewhere, watching, waiting, perhaps choosing another victim.

Turning away to start back down the hall to view more videos, he shivered. Every time he pictured the serial killer's victims, those thoughts included Emily Zwalt, as if her presence was a necessary element of the overall crime spree.

He hoped it wasn't. He prayed it wasn't. Because at this point he cared way too much, and the more he thought about everything that had been happening, the harder it was for him to separate her from impending tragedy.

FIFTEEN

To Emily's disappointment, Chief Rowlings had ordered pizzas for the whole station, so her plan to dine in private with Noah had failed. All she could do was accept the way her idea had blossomed and share the meal with everybody, which meant inviting Noah into the station break room with the others and acting as if she didn't mind.

Funny how things turned out, wasn't it? she thought. This was the perfect opportunity for him to meet other officers as well as the dispatchers and their maintenance people. That had to be to his advantage, so what was bugging her?

Everything and nothing. She flipped open the lids of all the pizza boxes and found mushrooms on every variety, so she grabbed a fork and started flipping them off a large slice for Noah.

He appeared at her elbow and leaned over. "What are you doing?"

"Taking off the mushrooms for you."

"That's not necessary."

"Just trying to help."

"My arm and my back may hurt, but I don't need to be coddled," he said flatly.

Suddenly she felt foolish, so she thrust the paper plate at him. "Here."

Turning to the pizzas, she grabbed a slice from the closest one, carried it back to her desk in the squad room instead of staying with the others and plopped down with a sigh. Confusion was rare for her. So was embarrassment, yet she'd been feeling plenty of that lately.

I'm not the problem. He is, she told herself with conviction. It had been years since she'd experienced feelings of disquiet when dealing with people, men or women, and to be so flustered around Noah was more than a bother. It was troubling. Very troubling.

"It's also dangerous," Emily murmured under her breath. Losing her cool, for whatever reason, was not only unprofessional, but it put herself and others at risk. The ability to compartmentalize and set aside distractions while functioning as a police officer was part gift, part learned behavior. Lots of people didn't have that ability, but she had what it took. Her instructors at the police academy had told her so. Chief Rowlings had commended her, too.

A lack of ability wasn't the problem, she knew. A lack of staying isolated, however, was. Oh, she had plenty of friends in a casual sense. There were her fellow officers as well as her church family to call upon if she had a need, but they weren't the kinds of friends who made her want to bare her heart or completely trust their discretion. That was a sad facet of her withdrawal after Jake's death. Had she been that way before? She didn't think so, although she'd always kept a rein on her emotions, particularly in public.

A deep voice close by startled her. A fork appeared in her peripheral vision. Her head snapped around. "What?"

Noah gave her a lopsided smile. "If I let you play with my food again, will you come back to the party?"

"I was just trying to please."

"Which can be a detriment in most relationships," Noah said. "I told you I like it when you're yourself."

Bristling because she was both embarrassed and put off, she scowled at him. "Nobody likes it when I'm too honest."

"I do."

The smile he continued to display only served to antagonize her further. "No, you don't. You questioned my motives the first time we met, and you haven't stopped."

"About becoming a cop? Maybe. But you criticized my profession, too."

"That doesn't make you right and me wrong." The urge to go on was almost uncontrollable. If Noah's grin hadn't waned and his countenance saddened, she might have.

He placed his plate on her desk and walked away. Emily could tell he was headed back down the hallway to watch more videos. Imagining herself running after him to apologize for being so cross and seeing the return of his smile, she stood fast. Life had been so much simpler before Noah had come back to Paradise. At least, *her* life had.

Noah concluded that the most sensible thing to do was finish his stint at the police station and resume his real job ASAP. All he had to do was figure out how to do that while continuing to look out for Emily, which was clearly impossible.

The thought of her being in danger for the rest of her career was enough to tie his guts in a knot. Knowing that most of her official responses would be for nuisance calls didn't do much to calm him down, either. It wasn't the run-of-the-mill stuff that got cops killed. It was the occasional anomaly, the summons that led to mortal danger.

"I'm as bad as she is, for opposite reasons," he muttered. While Emily was too brash, he was letting his imagination rule his senses and shut down his logical thinking. Most cops retired after long terms of service, and they deserved every day of health and happiness that waited for them.

So, did he really trust God, or was he going to make himself miserable by doubting?

The images on the laptop screen continued to pass. Noah's subconscious caught a slightly familiar face. He jerked. Stabbed at Pause on the touch screen and slowly backed up the images until he saw things clearly.

Was that her? The newest victim? Had she been there too, with the blondes he remembered? Perhaps her darker hair was why he hadn't noticed her, although she was pretty enough. He corrected himself on his way to the door. She *had been* pretty.

Starting to whip around the corner into the hallway, he almost collided with Emily. "Whoa!"

"What is it?" she asked immediately. "Did you find her?"

"I think so." Noah led the way to the laptop. "That looks like her, right?"

Emily leaned down to peer at the screen. "Maybe. We'll have to let our facial recognition software match the face."

"Why didn't you use that in the first place?"

"Takes too long."

"How long will it be before we can tell if this is… Kristin, did you say?"

"Kirsty. Kirsty McAdams. She's been working as a cook at the Paradise Café. I'm surprised you haven't met her."

"Maybe that's why she looked a little familiar. I cut through the café kitchen when I was chasing after Buddy the other day."

"Interesting."

"Not to me, it isn't. You're grasping at straws."

Because Emily appeared to be thinking, Noah waited for her to defend herself. When she said, "You may have a point," he had to smother a grin. She went on. "I had planned to go over the clues that pertain to you when we shared lunch but, as you know, that plan was derailed."

"How about supper? Late, so I have time to do some actual casework for Max?"

"I guess that will do. Where? Back at the safe house?"

Astounded by her unqualified agreement, Noah arched his eyebrows. "It would be a lot easier for me if we didn't leave town again. I suppose a meal at the Paradise Café is a bad idea since Kirsty worked there."

"Right. And restaurants in Springfield are out. I can't get too far away when I'm on call. We all are until this killer is caught. The safe house would do but I really hate to go back there, don't you?"

In unison, they said, "My place?" and laughed.

"Can you cook?" Noah asked.

Emily was grinning at him. "Thank you."

"For what?"

"For not assuming I'm a wonderful cook because I'm a woman."

"Hey, I'm pretty good in the kitchen, and I'm a guy."

The blush rising on her cheeks pleased him even more when she said, "Yeah, I noticed."

* * *

Armed with a file about the crime spree in a tote and her service weapon concealed in a holster at her waist, Emily parked in front of Noah's apartment. She wasn't surprised to see that he'd chosen a small, simple place, probably since he wasn't planning to stay long. She'd prayed about the image she was projecting by visiting him alone and felt assured that a business dinner was certainly not out of the ordinary, nor should it be subject to rumor.

The street was fairly well lit, and the two-story brick building had a bright yellow vapor light directly above the main door. Notes on his apartment number weren't necessary. She remembered his every word, down to each pause and facial expression, which was handy but also disquieting.

Cicadas buzzed in the bushes, their calls starting at varying intervals before joining into a mutual chorus. Once the weather cooled more, the night would return to a comfortable silence.

She shivered as she approached. The insects had stopped buzzing. No night birds sang. When she scanned her surroundings and saw nothing out of the ordinary, she told herself she was being paranoid, then huffed. "Yeah, you're only paranoid if nobody is out to get you."

There was an intercom next to the entrance. Emily buzzed 201 and waited. Noah didn't answer, and the door didn't release.

She pushed the button again. Nothing.

Shadows shifted. Emily shaded her eyes from the distortion of the porch light and strained to pick out details in the distance. Being jumpy wasn't like her. On the other hand, neither was standing under a bright light and making a target of herself.

Rather than draw her gun, she reached up and pressed every button on the intercom, one after the other.

The latch clicked. Emily prepared to enter. She was half turned when the door was jerked open and she almost fell through.

A strong hand grabbed her arm. Held her. She swung the tote in self-defense.

"Hey!" Noah fended off the blow. "It's me."

"Why didn't you let me in?"

"Nobody else has tried to visit me here. I guess the system is broken. I looked out and saw your car, so I came down to see why you hadn't rung." He began to shut the door behind her.

Emily heard a strange thunking noise just as the heavy wooden door closed. "Wait. What was that?"

"What was what?"

"I heard something. Outside. Didn't you?"

"I wasn't really paying attention."

"Well, I was." She handed him the heavy canvas tote and closed her fingers around the grip of her gun. Her other hand reached for the doorknob. Turned it. Eased open the door while staying out of sight.

There it was. Right at eye level. The height of her head. A rush of adrenaline made her tremble. She drew her gun, ready for a further attack.

Behind her, Noah asked, "What's wrong?" and Emily stepped aside slightly. "Look for yourself."

"Is that a..."

Breathless, she filled in the rest of his sentence. "Yeah. It's a knife. Call the police and report another attack."

The cozy meal Noah had planned ended up being a buffet that included the two police officers who responded to Emily's request for backup. Cal Dodge, he knew. The other man, rookie Larry Mullins, looked barely old enough to have graduated high school.

Emily had met them at the outer door. "Be careful when you bag that knife," she warned. "I want prints preserved."

Noah didn't like Dodge's tone when he replied, "We know our job, Zwalt," but didn't defend her. If he wasn't willing to let her coddle him, he couldn't very well treat her as if she needed his input all the time. As for pulling her in the door the way he had, he credited divine intervention. It made no difference how large or small the knife was. The intent was clear. Somebody had meant to harm Emily.

Dodge and Mullins had come up to Noah's apartment after examining the yard and finding no more clues. To say that Noah was disappointed was an understatement, but he made the best of the situation and offered refreshments.

They'd finished the cheese and crackers he'd provided, and each had left with a plastic container of fresh fruit and a slice of the cheesecake he'd bought to share with Emily for dessert. Closing the apartment door behind them was a relief.

"I had planned to broil a couple of steaks for us," Noah told Emily. "Are you hungry?"

"Not after all those appetizers," she said, smiling. "Why don't you save the steaks for another time?"

He had to grin. "Another time? Do you mean that?"

"Sure. We all have to eat."

Although he would have preferred that she emphasize being with him instead of merely sharing a meal, he was willing to take what he could get at this point.

"Well, at least they left enough dessert for us to enjoy later tonight."

Placing the tote on the kitchen table, she waited while Noah cleared away the remaining food, then started to display pictures from the board at the safe house as well as unused pads of lined paper.

There were two dining chairs. She sat in one while he pulled up the other, noticing that she didn't seem to mind his nearness one bit. With his right arm resting on the back of her chair, Noah leaned closer. "What are we doing now?"

"We're each going to make two lists. One will be for the victims of the serial killer. The second is for the other attacks, like the knife in your door. Then we'll see if we agree, and if we don't, why we don't."

"I'd think the results would be the same."

Emily leaned her head to one side and pressed her lips together as she looked at him. "That's one of the things I want to see. The similarities don't interest me nearly as much as the differences do." She pushed a pad and pen at him. "Here. And no peeking. Use the photos for reference so you won't forget anything."

Following her instructions had sounded easy until he tried it. Starting with the murders, he listed the three blonde women, Charity, Annie and Kit. Unsure about Vangie or the latest, Kirsty, he switched to the second list. That one, he headed with Buddy's call drawing him to the park, then added the threat while he sat in the police car. There was no forgetting the first rifle shot, either, of course, but should it tie to the Roskov woman or to Buddy or to threats against the police?

Noah leaned back, thoughtful. "I see the problem now."

"Thought you might."

"Where do you think the first rifle attack in the park belongs? Was that from the serial killer?"

Emily shrugged. "Beats me. Put it wherever you choose, and we'll sort it out later."

He picked up the pen and studied the crime reports strewn on the table. "Can I move these into chronological order?"

"I mixed them up on purpose," Emily said. "Let's work with them this way at first, then arrange things better."

"Okay, if you say so."

"I'm going to add Buddy running from me at the café."

"Fine."

"Then the knifing at your place, right?" When she stayed silent, he jotted that down, then started to put Laura Bright on the second list before changing his mind due to the hospital attacks on her and Officer Anderson and starting to cross out her name.

Emily intervened with a hand on his. "Leave that as your first conclusion. Duplicate if you're not sure." She pulled a face. "I'm not sure, either."

"Okay." Mulling over all that had occurred, Noah understood why the police were confused. He'd been involved in most of the secondary crimes, and he was mixed up, too.

"Has anybody managed to interview Vangie yet?" he asked, getting ready to add her name to one of the lists.

"No. Not yet. Her mental health is in question, and they're afraid to push her too hard."

"Okay." Pen poised, Noah added her name to both lists, too. At this point he had as many doubles as he did singles.

The incident at the police station was easier to decide

about. That couldn't have had anything to do with the serial killer, could it? That shooter had simply wanted to damage police property. Unless…

He laid aside the pen and crossed his arms, noticing the pain that caused in his ribs and back. "I'm seeing something," he said pensively.

"Yes?" Emily swiveled to face him, covering her own lists as she did so. "What's that?"

"Me," Noah said. "I know I'm innocent, and I hope you think so, too, but there isn't one of these crimes that doesn't touch my life in some way."

"Thank you."

"For what?"

"For admitting what I've been trying to tell you ever since I saw you in the park. It all leads back to you."

"And to you," he argued. "Remember the knife in my door tonight."

"Thrown here, if you'll recall."

He rose so quickly he almost toppled the chair, starting to pace as he considered the undeniable connections. "What can I do? How can I stop this?"

"We're already doing it," Emily said calmly. She gestured at the empty chair. "Come on. Sit back down and finish your lists so we can discuss the places where we may disagree."

"That's why you wanted to do this with me, isn't it? You wanted to prove to me that it was my fault."

"Not at all. You aren't responsible if some unbalanced individual focuses on your personal life any more than I'm responsible for criminals who get off with light sentences."

"Not the same at all," Noah argued. "It's beyond my control if somebody has it in for me or my friends."

The expression on Emily's face could only be described as triumph as his mind carried that thought through to its natural conclusion. She was still blaming defense attorneys, not him necessarily, but those in his profession. She might be willing to excuse him for unknowingly bringing about tragedy, but she wasn't ready to admit how much good his work did in the grand scheme of things.

Well, he knew better. Families had been preserved, relationships between parent and adult child restored, and on and on. Admittedly he was sometimes wrong. No one could claim unfailing discernment. His goal wasn't perfection. It was to provide a second chance to people who had given up on themselves, on life in general.

Returning to the table, he glanced over his lists, added the knife throwing and drew a line across the paper. *The end. No more*, Noah prayed silently. *God help me to figure this out and stop it. Please. Soon.*

SIXTEEN

Emily slid her list next to Noah's and discovered that the only places where they totally disagreed were times that had directly involved her. They both thought the Roskov murder was part of the serial killer's work. She'd put Laura Bright in the random category while Noah had decided she, too, was part of the crime spree.

Pointing with her pen she asked, "Why this one? Is it because she's blonde?"

Noah nodded. "That, and the secondary attack at the hospital."

"So that's why you put Anderson in the serial column?"

"Yes. There has to be a connection, right?"

"Maybe." Pensive, she let her mind delve deeper. "However, he's also a uniformed officer."

"So, put him on both lists."

"That's becoming another problem," Emily said. "We have an awful lot of overlap."

"Yeah, I noticed."

"Okay." She began to shift the photos and police reports that lay before them, starting with the crimes that had been committed before Noah's arrival in Paradise.

When she looked over at him, he was frowning.

"This is pretty solid," he said, pointing to the three blondes, "including the body in the park."

"Which is a direct link to you," Emily said.

"Yes. It is. Which is why I put Laura Bright on the same list. She fits all the criteria."

"Not college," Emily reminded him.

"No, but we were acquainted. And that attack happened right here in town. If you only consider my college days, you can't include anybody since."

"What about Vangie?"

Noah seemed frustrated. "I have no idea. I suppose she should go with the college crowd. So should Kirsty if you can find any connection to my past, although she may have been targeted because of Buddy."

"What's your assessment of Buddy?" Emily asked. "We know he, or someone pretending to be him, lured you to the park."

"Personally, I think it was him. I just can't figure out why."

"You don't see him as a murderer, do you?"

"No, do you?"

Emily shook her head. "No. He comes from an odd family, but I don't think he has the guts or the intelligence to get away with murder, especially not repeatedly."

It had occurred to her that they might be dealing with more than one killer, but she hesitated to put that idea into Noah's head. If he happened to think of it, however, she planned to share her conclusions.

With a deep, noisy sigh, Noah leaned back and laced his fingers behind his head, elbows out. "What if…"

"Go ahead."

"Naw, it's silly."

"Nothing is silly if it brings us closer to solving these crimes."

"Okay." Resting his elbows on the table he slowly nodded. "Suppose some of these crimes have nothing to do with either list? I mean, what if we're including too much in this investigation?"

"We?"

"Okay, you then. Are there any events that could be scratched off the lists?"

"Such as?"

"I don't know. You're the professional. You tell me."

This was what she'd been waiting for. "Okay, but if you disagree, I want you to speak up."

"I will."

"Suppose there's no division. Suppose these crimes all trace back to one source."

Shaking his head, Noah frowned at the lists. "I'm not buying that. Some are clearly personal violence, and others were carried out from a distance."

"Like the shot at you in the car?"

"All the shooting at the police cars. Are there ballistic similarities, or are we dealing with different firearms?"

She liked the way his mind was working, so she stayed silent in the hopes he'd take his ideas further. When he continued to puzzle over it, she finally spoke. "What if we divide the lists that way?"

"Which way? By sources of attacks or the personal angle?"

"We can try both." Emily gave him a slight smile. "By the way, your list is incomplete. You left out the kitchen knife stuck in my pillow."

"Did I? Sorry. There's been so much going on I forgot." Noah returned her smile and arched his eyebrows. "It's been a little hairy around here lately."

"Ya think?"

He huffed, said, "Yeah. I think," and tore off the used sheets of paper to start again. "So, how was Charity Roskov killed? I'd assumed she was shot, but I never asked."

Emily's smile faded, and her gaze fixed on the lists. "No, not shot," she said quietly. "She was hit over the head like I was, but the thing that killed her was a sharp blade. The coroner estimates it to have been fairly short."

"Like the one in my door tonight?"

"Yes," she said with a barely perceptible shudder. "Just like that one."

Noah managed to stay focused on their mutual task enough to adjust his notes accordingly. When he combined the knife attacks and eliminated anything involving firearms, it was necessary to also consider anomalies, like Laura Bright and the assailant who rammed the cleaning cart into Emily. The mere thought of that incident brought the urge to embrace her again.

Instead, he leaned back and asked, "Where do you see Laura's place in all this? Are we sure her husband's innocent?"

"She says he is," Emily replied. "At this point, I think we should assume she's telling the truth, because the events that followed fit better into the serial killer scenario."

"Who came up with that idea in the first place?"

Emily looked a bit puzzled. "I think it was Chief Rowlings. It wasn't a hard conclusion to reach since we haven't had any killings in Paradise for years. Then all of a sudden, we're inundated."

"Any word from the FBI on the clues?"

She shook her head. "Sadly, no. I'm hoping ballistics on the rifle bullets will turn up something they can trace. If they do make a connection and it includes other states, they'll come in whether we request them or not."

Feeling his back muscles tighten at the thought of being hit so hard and escaping death by inches, Noah stretched with a flex of his shoulders. There was no doubt, in his opinion, that divine intervention had saved him. After all, his head had been exposed as well as his lower torso. Any number of errant shots could have ended his life, vest or no vest.

He pushed himself back to the task at hand. "Suppose we divide these attacks by method rather than victims? What happens then?"

"We get about the same result," Emily said. "Except for the incapacitating head wounds. Those were less predictable. I got hit in the park the night you found the body."

"That I do remember," Noah said, laying his hand over hers where it rested atop the pile of police reports. "What happened, exactly? Did you think whoever hit you was going to come for you with a knife, too?"

When her head snapped around, eyes widening, Noah's heart leaped. She'd recalled something new, thanks to him, and he was so thankful he was temporarily speechless.

"There were *two* of them," Emily announced, almost shouting. It took both hands to shuffle through the police reports, so she pulled away from Noah. "I know I must have mentioned it. I was groggy and my head was splitting, but there's no way I would have forgotten that."

He leaned closer to read while she scanned the original paperwork regarding her injury. It listed time, circumstances, responding officers and little else.

Emily slapped her palm down on the report as if the piece of paper was responsible for the omission. "I don't believe it. I know I told Cal."

"Maybe he figured you'd add more details later, and with everything that's been going on, it slipped your mind."

"It shouldn't have."

"I hate to be the one to break this to you, Emily, but nobody's perfect." Pausing, he smiled tenderly. "Not even the smartest, best-educated, most dedicated cop in Paradise, Missouri."

Muttering, "Two, there were two," over and over, Emily pulled out her cell phone.

"Who are you calling?"

"Rowlings," she said flatly. "I have to tell him."

"I understand," Noah said. "Just remember, you'd been knocked out and were probably concussed at the time."

"That's no excuse."

Frustrated, he studied her expression while she amended her incident report in the call to her chief. *Here we go again*, Noah thought, wondering how Emily got through daily life if she assumed blame for everything that went wrong. Just when he'd been hoping she'd be able to forgive herself, forgive God, for her great loss, here she was, taking on unwarranted guilt again.

Ending the short call, she pocketed her phone. The revelation of the second man had clearly hit her hard, because her shoulders were slumped and her eyes misty.

Noah chanced touching her hand again and was rewarded by a wan smile. "Thanks," she said.

"For what?"

"Supporting me in spite of my mistakes."

"That's what friends do," Noah said softly. "I'm pretty sure your boss isn't upset with you."

"He didn't sound like he was."

"See? He knows you're human, too." Noah so wanted to add that anybody could err at any time, including attorneys and judges, but he kept that to himself. For the present, it was enough to feel thankful that Emily was beginning to admit fallibility in her own actions. Forgiving others would come later. At least, he hoped so.

And in the meantime, he thought, glancing at the papers strewn across the table, they had to rethink each crime with the supposition that more than one person had participated. Doing that was going to change everything. He had already wondered if the knifings and shootings were separate. Now that they had to assume multiple participants, the field was widening.

Emily pulled away, pushed back her chair and stood. "Excuse me. I need to go splash cold water on my face."

"Sure. I'll make us a fresh pot of coffee and get out the cheesecake."

"Cheesecake? Now? How is that supposed to help?"

With a sigh and benevolent smile, Noah rose. "It'll have to do, I'm afraid. I'm all out of chocolate ice cream."

Emily threw her hands into the air as she faced him, let out a loud "Aargh," and left the room.

Laughter was inappropriate, he knew, but he did allow himself a grin.

There was a fine line between lifting her spirits and causing a distraction, a line he was balancing on as if it were the blade of a knife. He also had to keep reminding himself that he wasn't the one making the ultimate decisions here. God was. If, as he believed, divine providence had brought him back to Paradise and back into Emily's life, then he had to trust the future to the Savior who had lifted him out of a dysfunctional childhood and molded him into someone whose goal it was to help the downtrodden. Oh, he had to also make a living, sure, but time and trials had shown that that would come if he lived according to the principles Max had taught him and reached out to others who had yet to see the light.

It struck Noah that it might be easier to reach someone who did *not* share his basic faith than it was going to be to reach Emily. As long as she continued to think that God had failed or abandoned her, she was going to remain miserable.

The problem he and so many others had was grasping even a smidgen of truth about the God of the Universe. People tended to think in temporal terms and put the same limits on their Heavenly Father that they themselves had. Nothing could be further from the truth.

By the time Noah had brewed the coffee and served the cheesecake onto small plates, he knew what he needed to do next. A different list was required, one that enumerated all the times when his or Emily's lives might have been lost, yet were preserved. Facts spoke for themselves. He and Emily had both escaped death over and over in the past few days.

Hindsight provided enough instances in his childhood alone, but Noah decided to concentrate on the files they'd been working with. He titled his special list *Close* and began to write, starting with the mild stroke Max had suffered that had drawn him back to Paradise.

By the time Emily returned, Noah had worked his way down to the knife stuck in his door and the way he had chosen to pull her inside because the entry intercom had failed. That alone was totally out of character, yet he'd done it.

Smiling, she joined him and took a sip from the mug he'd brought for her. "Oh, it's hot."

"Steam is your first clue."

She took a playful swing at him with the back of her free hand. "Duh. What are you doing?"

"Making another list. Just for us."

"Us?" This sip was taken more cautiously.

Noah nodded. "Uh-huh. I thought it might be good to make a list of all the times when we didn't die."

"Um." Another sip. "We don't have nearly enough paper for that."

"I'm beginning to agree," Noah said, smiling amiably. "For all the times we can name, there have to be dozens we miss seeing."

"Thousands." Emily set aside her mug and picked up a fork.

"You really believe that, don't you?" Waiting, Noah prayed for the reply he wanted.

"Yes. It's an exercise in futility to try to write it all down, so you may as well go back to the work we came here to do."

One of the important things he'd come to Paradise to do was, in his mind and heart, helping Emily to heal her personal scars. Did he dare say so, or was it too soon?

He smiled at her, pushed the tablet away and forked up a bite of dessert. The time would come when it was undeniably right to speak more about trust and forgiveness.

An icy shiver zinged up his spine, passing through the center of the enormous bruise and triggering needles of pain. *Please, Lord, help me keep her safe.*

No holy voice from Heaven echoed the answer, but

Noah knew. He would do all he could, but in the grand scheme of things, Emily's well-being was no more in his hands than the ultimate fate of her late fiancé had been in hers.

That concept was hard to accept because he liked feeling in control, but the same thing he'd told her applied to him. All they could do in any given situation was their very best.

What happened as a result was not in their hands.

It never had been.

SEVENTEEN

Before they'd parted for the evening, Emily had tried several times to get a good look at Noah's list of narrow escapes. When he'd noticed her interest, however, he'd crumpled up the paper and tossed the wad into a wastebasket. The letter of the law told her that anything thrown away could be picked up. Her moral compass wasn't quite as sure.

Compromising meant digging in the trash while Noah was present, so she retrieved the paper and smoothed it out. Most of the instances listed were familiar to her. What was surprising was his conclusion that God had sent him back to his home town to be of special assistance to *her.* If that notion had crossed her mind in the past, she wasn't aware of it. Until now. Could he be right? Was that why everything seemed to be coordinating in an effort to throw them together?

Emily raised her glance to meet his, and she smiled. "Interesting."

"My opinion, that's all."

She sighed. "You may be right. I hesitate to see myself as needing any help, but without your input, we might not have made the college connection yet."

"True. Thanks for not pinning it all on my past."

Arching her eyebrows, she smiled. "It may still turn out that way, you know."

"I do. And if it does, I'll accept the truth."

Watching Noah stretch again and seeing his faraway look, she waited. When he did speak, it surprised her. "Suppose Buddy was the first guy who ran into you in the park, and his accomplice was the real killer?"

Emily shook her head. "I don't know about that. I mean, why would Buddy Corrigan want to kill your client when you're his lawyer, too?"

"Beats me. Maybe Buddy was just the fall guy, same as me. Have you looked into who his friends are?"

"I'm sure someone has. If there was any connection to that victim and one of Buddy's friends, it should have come to light by now."

"Not necessarily," Noah argued. "Her murder occurred most recently."

"Yes, but we haven't released information on the supposedly connected crimes. Whoever was responsible wouldn't know how to make it a copycat killing."

A look of sadness washed over Noah to the extent that Emily laid her hand over his. "What?"

Lips pressed into a thin line, he shook his head slowly, pensively. "Listen to us. We're talking about the loss of life as if it was no more important than whether or not it had rained yesterday. That's terrible."

"It's necessary in order to keep a clear head," she countered. "Getting too emotionally involved can skew conclusions."

Noah looked directly into her eyes and said, "There. That. Do you see what I've been trying to tell you?" Pausing, he swallowed hard. "Your feelings are keeping you from clearly seeing events in your past, and you're assuming personal blame that you don't deserve."

"No."

"Yes, you are."

She felt his other hand covering the one she'd had resting over his. His touch was warm, comforting, and the depth of his gaze held her captive. It had never been a question of not understanding his point of view. The problem had been her own reluctance to seeing how it might apply to her. Letting go of guilt would certainly make her feel better, but was it right? Was Noah right? Had she formed a warped picture of loss that was holding her back?

Holding tightly to denial was more comfortable than a change of heart. "I know what happened. I was there, remember?"

"And how many others have you interviewed whose memories of traumatic moments contradicted known facts?"

"That has nothing to do with me. I'm a trained observer."

"Who cared about a victim."

"Of course I did."

"Then how can you say for sure whether anything you could have done would have saved or cost a life? In your mind, you know better."

Emily's head was spinning as Noah's words warred with her previous conclusions. Truth to tell, as the years had passed, certain details had become emphasized while others had faded until they no longer mattered. Professional studies had shown her that this process was the way the brain brought inner healing. If a person allowed it, she added.

She spoke softly, sorrowfully. "It's hard to let go."

"But necessary. You've been stuck in a prison of your own making, serving a sentence you don't deserve."

"I wish I could believe you."

"Never mind me. Believe God. Trust Him in all things. There's no halfway in and halfway out. You either accept the life you've been given and do the best with what you have, or you don't."

"It's not that simple."

Noah pulled her to her feet, put his arms around her and held her close. Emily could hear his heart beating as she laid her cheek on his chest and surrendered to the peace he was offering.

"No, it's not simple," he said. "But *we* are. Suppose the reason we don't understand why things happen is because we're incapable of sharing the full wisdom of our Heavenly Father."

"Meaning, I'll never know for sure if I could have done more to save Jake?"

"Exactly. It can be frustrating. We all try to figure out what God means when things happen that are beyond our control. Release comes when we accept His will as what's best, even if we disagree to the depths of our hearts."

Although Emily didn't remember putting her arms around his waist, there they were. She tightened the embrace. Sensed an increase in the speed of his pulse. Heard him release a ragged breath and realized she might be hurting him.

An effort to loosen her hug for his comfort was countered with a firmer hold from Noah. His voice rumbled, and she felt his breath against her hair when he said, "Stay a minute more. Think about it. 'All things work together for good.'"

Emily finished the verse from the book of Romans. "'To those who are called according to His purpose.'"

"You are," Noah said quietly.

No reply but one would suffice, so Emily said, "So are you."

Nothing could have pleased him more, Noah thought, except maybe for her to let him kiss her. It didn't take a genius to see that this wasn't the right time for that. Their relationship had made an enormous leap in the past few moments, and he wasn't about to spoil it. Merely holding her and hearing her accept his career choices was enough. For now.

Emily had just started to loosen her grip and lean away when her cell phone rang. Reluctantly, Noah let her go.

"Zwalt here," she answered. "Yes, sir."

That told Noah her chief was on the line, and he wondered if cops ever really got a day off. It was beginning to look as if they did not.

Listening to Rowlings speaking, Emily nodded. "Yes, he's here. We're at his place going over the cases and trying to come up with conclusions." She frowned, then looked at Noah and told the chief, "I'm sure we can. Hold on."

Noah frowned. "Not another killing?"

"No. They captured a man trying to sneak into Vangie Mead's hospital room in Memphis." She held her phone to show Noah a grainy photo taken from a security camera. "Do you know him?"

"I don't think so."

"In that case, are you up for a quick drive to Memphis? Just there and back. You won't miss much work."

"I guess so." To tell the truth, he was excited about

having the opportunity to spend more time with her but figured it was better to refrain from pumping a fist in the air and cheering the way he wanted to.

"First thing in the morning okay?" Emily asked Rowlings.

Noah saw her nod and was thankful he'd get some sleep. Running on adrenaline was fine for a crisis situation, but the lack of proper rest caught up eventually.

She ended the call and pocketed the phone. "I'll pick you up at 9:00 a.m. tomorrow if that's okay. We can grab breakfast on the way."

"I'll be through my first pot of coffee by then," Noah said. "It'll be faster if we go straight there."

"That works for me."

Nothing about her facial expression was easy to read, but Emily didn't look as happy about their road trip as he'd expected, so he added, "We can stop to eat if that's what you want."

"No. The faster the better." She was gathering the loose sheets of paper into a stack and stuffing them back into her tote as if the forms themselves had caused offense.

If Noah had had the slightest inkling of why her mood had flipped so fast, he would have asked an appropriate question, but he didn't have a clue. Thinking along those lines made him smile slightly. Clues to crimes might be confusing, but entry into the mind of this woman could be akin to wandering a vast wilderness with no map, no GPS. In Emily's case, the struggle was worse, he concluded, because he already cared far too much about her.

He'd travel with her armed, of course. Restrictions against his use of a gun were many, yet he felt a distinct need to be prepared. Concern for her welfare was why he'd suggested a trip uninterrupted by stops. The less time they spent standing still, the fewer opportunities there would be for another sneak attack.

Shrugging his shoulders, he followed Emily all the way to the main door. "I'll walk you out."

"That's not necessary."

"Humor me."

A wry smile preceded her reply. "I hate to tell you this, Noah, but I have been humoring you ever since we met again."

"No reason to stop now, then," he countered as he reached for the door handle.

"Wait." Emily barred his way with an outstretched arm. "Since you insist on sticking close, you need to begin acting appropriately."

Several quips occurred to Noah. He kept them to himself and stood back so she could open the door the way she wanted.

It swung back slowly as Emily scanned the yard and street. Then she tilted her head slightly and gasped.

Noah reacted instinctively and slipped in front of her. She didn't resist, which was out of character. So was her rapid breathing. The threat she'd seen fell at his eye level so he spotted it instantly.

A note was pinned to the center of the wooden door with a knife identical to the one that had been thrown earlier in the evening.

He started to reach for it. Emily stopped him. "No. Don't touch that."

"I just want to read it."

"I said, *no*. That's evidence, and this could be an ambush."

Despite her warning, Noah leaned out, leaving the door ajar so he could quickly return, and stood firm against Emily's tugs on his arm.

"They won't attack me," he told her.

"How do you know?"

"Because of the note," he replied, wishing he could rip it loose.

"Why?"

Noah stepped back inside and eased the door closed. "Call your buddies at the station and tell them to get back out here ASAP."

"What does the note say?"

A deep sigh preceded his answer. "To paraphrase, 'Stay away from him or you'll die too.'"

As Emily made the report to her station, Noah stood close by, thunderstruck by the proof that he was the root cause of the fatalities. Yes, he had suspected a connection, but nothing like this. Nothing so blatantly stated. Women he had barely known had died because of him. So apparently had at least one of his clients. That was appalling.

Worse yet, whoever had it in for him had seen his blossoming interest in Emily and was now targeting her. The fact that most earlier victims had been blondes had had nothing to do with their demise. Nothing at all. They could have had any hair and eye color and been in just as much jeopardy.

Acting on instinct, Noah slipped an arm around Emily's shoulders and drew her closer. There was no denying how much he cared for her, nor was he about to back off and rely on wishful thinking to protect her from this threat. He'd gotten her into this mess, and he was going to see it through.

"I'm so sorry," she said sadly once she'd ended her call. "I kept hoping the connection to you was coincidental."

"Yeah, so was I." Noah felt her leaning against him slightly and tightened his grip on her shoulders. "If I'd dreamed my presence would pose a threat to you, or to anyone, I'd have kept my distance."

"It wouldn't have mattered," Emily argued. "Whoever left this threat has to be mentally unbalanced. Anything could have set off a reaction."

"I didn't lead any women on, if that's what you're thinking. I'm not like that."

"I know you're not."

Sounds of sirens in the distance had been growing louder. When they ended at the apartment, Noah let go of Emily and stepped back. His fault. This was his fault. Although he was certain he'd taken no part in whatever trauma was causing some poor soul to target women he'd once shown an interest in, he still felt a sense of doom, of guilt.

That had to be similar to Emily's reaction to the loss of her fiancé. Now he did understand. And he empathized.

Renewed purpose filled him. Of all the reasons he'd given for his work, this was one of the most crucial. Innocent people who had been wrongly accused would always be important to him, but now he could see another facet of crime. Besides the perpetrator and his or her victims, there were the families and friends suffering on both sides.

He couldn't make their grief disappear any more than he could heal Emily's heart without leaving a scar, but he could do his best to ameliorate their pain by bringing the truly guilty to justice.

Starting with his stalker, Noah added firmly. This was one time when he'd gladly agree with whoever led the eventual prosecution team.

Only first, they had to find this killer and assemble enough evidence to convince a judge and jury.

EIGHTEEN

Dawn came too early to suit Emily, thanks to the on-scene investigation of the threatening note. She yawned as she donned her uniform. Three mugs of coffee later, she slipped into a properly fitted bulletproof vest, checked her gun before holstering it, and headed for Noah's.

Evidence from the night before had been sent directly to the FBI, and although she knew their labs were state-of-the-art, she also feared her clues would get bogged down in the overload the bureau dealt with constantly.

She and her chief had discussed canceling this trip after last night's threat. Thankfully, her appeal to continue had prevailed. She trusted Noah's innocence and was confident she could protect him in spite of the sniper who had come so close in the past. Proper preparation gave them an edge over times before when they had known less about the killer and her motives.

Emily was certain they were dealing with a female, although she also recalled the possibility that there might be a team of two or more pulling off the serial murders. One of those people could easily be male, so focusing exclusively on women would mean taking too narrow a view.

Her initial reaction to Noah turning down breakfast had been negative. Later, calmer thought had brought the realization that his choice made sense. The less they were exposed in public, the less danger they should encounter.

A bag of hot takeout food waited for him when he joined her in the patrol car and donned the new vest she handed him.

"Something smells good."

"My breakfast. You said you didn't need any, right?"

"I said we didn't need to stop to eat." He made a face as he clicked his seat belt. "That's not the same thing."

Emily laughed. "Then it's a good thing I bought enough for both of us."

"Seriously? You're not going to punish me for turning down a restaurant meal?"

"Nope. Dig in. There's extra bottled water in a cooler in the trunk if we want it, and one of these coffees is for you. Oh, and I got your phone back for you, too."

They were on the highway, headed southeast toward Memphis, before she brought up the case. "Have you given any more thought to past acquaintances?"

"I hardly think of anything else." Noah sipped his hot coffee. "Whatever is going on must have its roots in college because of the first victims. What I don't get is how my stalker can be close enough to me to know who my new clients are without my recognizing her or them."

"Were you actually looking before? It's possible you just didn't notice enough about the people around you. Most of us don't. We have our minds on a particular task, and the rest becomes background."

A quick glance his way told her he agreed, because he was nodding slowly.

"Speaking of which," Emily said as she checked her

rearview mirrors, "there's a chance we're being followed."

Noah whipped around so fast he sloshed coffee in spite of the lid on the cup. "Where? Which car?"

"A truck," she said, maintaining a steady speed. "Don't worry."

"Why not?" He was still scanning the traffic in their wake.

"Because we're not the only ones from the PPD out and about this morning. The chief put us in a regular patrol unit so we'd stand out on purpose. There's an unmarked car following us in the hopes we'll flush out your stalker."

"You should have told me I was bait."

Emily didn't like his accusatory tone. "You knew everything except that we'd have an escort."

"Still..."

Her hands were fisted on the wheel, her eyes narrowing as she reminded him, "It's not just you, Noah, it's me too."

Emily's matter-of-fact statement did not sit well with Noah, not well at all, particularly because he realized she was speaking the truth. She'd been the most recent focus of whoever was causing all the trouble, so it figured that she still would be.

The police radio sounded off, telling Emily to turn to a private channel. Noah held his breath as she complied and was relieved to hear that a pickup truck had been pulled over for following them, and its male occupant was being detained for questioning.

Nevertheless, it was a woman who was behind the attacks, right? Even if the man in the truck had been tracking them, there was still an accomplice to consider.

As soon as Emily was done using the radio, Noah asked her about it. "Do you think the guy in the truck is involved with the stalker?"

"Time will tell. There's no doubt he was on our trail or our escort wouldn't have pulled him over."

"Why didn't you stop when they did that? I might have recognized him."

Emily was smiling slightly, and if his gut hadn't been tied in a knot with worry, he would have smiled back at her.

"We had considered more than one vehicle might be involved, so it made sense to keep moving."

"Not with our protection stopped with that truck, it didn't."

"A calculated risk," she said. "I spotted the first tail. If there's a second, I'll see that, too. In the meantime, officers can be questioning the one they already have in custody. Chances are good that they'll have enough information for an arrest before we even get to Memphis."

"Really?" A part of Noah wanted to believe her. A more wary sense insisted she was being overly confident. This killer or stalker, or whatever they wanted to call her, was cagey and smart or she wouldn't have gotten away with so much already.

"Really." Emily switched the radio back to the open communications channel and seemed to relax as she drove.

Noah did not. Could not. He kept his eyes on the traffic mirrored behind them, occasionally turning in the seat for a direct view. Everything looked normal, although few drivers chose to pass them.

"Does a marked patrol car always hold up the flow of traffic like this?"

"Uh-huh." Emily grinned. "They're all worried I'll

pull them over for speeding. I could be driving thirty in a sixty-mile-an-hour zone and they'd still hang back there."

Noah huffed. "That would be funny if it wasn't making it hard for me to spot another tail."

"We'll see more once we get off the interstate. The bridge is open again, so we won't have to detour."

He knew she meant the eight-lane crossing of the Mississippi where the river divided Arkansas from Tennessee. Repairs had been ongoing for nearly a year.

"Could you take the alternate route anyway? That might help us pick out cars that do the same."

Her smile spread, and she flashed the grin at him. "Now you're starting to think like a cop."

Noah treated the comment as a joke and said, "There's no need to slander me," but in truth he was glad he'd had that idea and that Emily was taking his advice instead of discounting it because of the source.

She laughed, changed lanes and headed south to avoid the major river crossing. Most of the cars and trucks that had been behind them stayed on the highway while only one semi followed in their wake.

Noah continued to monitor everything around them until they reached their initial destination, the Tennessee Highway Patrol office. Emily got out first, clearly on her guard, and circled the car to escort him inside.

The next ten minutes were a blur, ending with his chance to view the man who had been apprehended in Vangie's hospital room. Noah's head was spinning. Delving deep into his memories, he came up with nothing, even when told the man's name. "I'm sorry. There's nothing about Nat Porter that seems even slightly familiar. As far as I know, I've never met him." Hearing

Emily sigh in disappointment, he met her gaze. "I'm sorry. I wish…"

"None of us want anything more from you than the truth," she said.

Noah stood back and listened as she thanked the sergeant who had arranged the viewing session, then followed her out of the station. "What now? Back to Paradise?"

"I think it would be a good idea if we stopped off to see Vangie since we're so close."

"Fine. I hardly remember her, either, but maybe something will come to me when we talk about college."

Emily paused next to the patrol car. "If it doesn't, don't beat yourself up. I know you're trying."

"Thanks." He got into the car.

As Emily slid behind the wheel, she added, "*Very* trying," followed by a light laugh.

"Very *funny*."

"I thought so. Don't you remember how you used to say that to me when we were kids?"

"Vaguely," he alibied. He did remember that, and more. In those days he'd been too young, too self-absorbed and unhappy to enjoy the simple gifts of God all around him, including Emily Zwalt. The more time he spent in Paradise as an adult, the more he came to realize how much potential joy he'd overlooked or rejected before. When he said his goodbyes to Paradise this time, he was going to feel more than relief. He was going to be truly sorry to leave.

The drive from the police station to the rehab facility where Vangie was staying didn't take long. Emily was glad to have a distraction for Noah, because he'd been brooding ever since failing to ID the suspect.

She parked in a reserved spot and preceded him into the nondescript building, surprised to find no need to key in a code to enter. No wonder they'd had an interloper. Still, that was actually a good thing since it had provided another suspect to question.

"We need to see Vangie Mead," Emily announced at the open door of the first office they came to, trusting her uniform and badge to get them admitted.

A woman in a business suit rose from behind the desk. "Ms. Mead is resting. She's been questioned too much already."

"We won't stay long," Emily promised. "We need to see if this gentleman recognizes her or if she knows him."

"Wait here."

While the manager spoke to nurses at a nearby station, Emily was visually checking the halls expecting trouble. It didn't surprise her to see that Noah was doing the same, although she would have preferred that he not stand so close. It appeared he was preparing to step between her and danger, so she quietly warned him off.

"You need to give me room to act if I need to," Emily whispered.

"Sorry. I didn't realize I was crowding you."

"Well, now you know, okay?"

"Yeah, sure."

Noah's reluctance to back off was palpable. Emily stood her ground, waiting. "More room, please. At least ten feet."

She saw his jaw clenching, but he complied.

One of the nurses stepped forward and motioned to them. "All right, you can go up. Second floor, room 217. If the patient acts overwhelmed, one of you will have to leave. She's pretty fragile after what happened the other day."

Emily nodded soberly. "We understand."

As she and Noah headed for the stairs, Emily explained, "I prefer this to the elevator. We can see farther ahead and behind us, as well."

"Don't you ever get tired of being paranoid?"

"Sure. Believe it or not, my job is usually pretty boring."

"Not since I showed up, it isn't."

She had to smile. "Now that you mention it."

"It will be nice when all this is over," he said.

"True." Except that would mean she'd have no good reasons to interact with him, she added to herself. There would undoubtedly be times when their paths crossed, of course, but nothing like this. Nothing like Noah's constant presence in her life, in her thoughts.

When had she morphed into someone who actually wanted to keep company with an attorney? she wondered, somewhat stunned. He'd gotten under her skin, hadn't he? Broken down the wall she'd so painstakingly erected around her most tender emotions and cleared away the fog of unwarranted blame.

The people who had released the criminal who had ended Jake's life were still on her villain list, but she had softened toward others who might hold the same job or bear the same kinds of responsibilities.

This was far from the right time to share her change of heart with Noah, but she would soon. Not that that would make a big difference in their shaky friendship. He obviously still didn't trust her to adequately defend herself or he wouldn't have hovered so close down in the lobby.

Habit caused Emily to pat her holster, checking her gun.

"Did you see something?" Noah asked.

"Simmer down. There's nothing wrong here." *Probably.*

Room 217 was on their left. Emily knocked on the door, paused, then pushed it open. The female guard she had expected to see in the hallway was seated by the patient's bed, reading a paperback. She stood.

Emily stepped into full view to identify herself and show her badge. "Paradise police," she said. "I have someone I'd like Ms. Mead to meet."

The middle-aged guard smiled at the patient in the bed. "Is that all right with you, Vangie? You don't have to, you know."

"I know." Pale, fine, ash-blond hair hung forward, partially masking her face. She combed it back with thin fingers. "It's all right. You can come in."

Following Emily into the room, Noah hung back until she stepped aside and gestured. "This is Noah Holden. Does he look familiar to you?"

"I—I don't know. I don't have my glasses."

The guard provided them. Vangie slipped them on and looked up.

"I recognize her now," Noah said. "It's the glasses."

"I'm sorry, but…" Vangie's eyes narrowed as she peered at him. "There may be a similarity to someone from my past, but I can't make the connection."

"The library," Noah said. "You volunteered at the college law library. That's where we met."

"If you say so."

"Is there anything else?" Emily asked them both, turning from Noah to Vangie and back. "Anything at all?"

"All I get is a vague impression," Vangie said.

"What about the people on the video you gave the

police? Do you think you recognized anybody in the background?"

"I wasn't looking at that," she replied. "They said they wanted pictures of Annie or Kit, so I gave them what I had." Tears began to trickle down her cheeks.

"I have my laptop with me in the car, and it's loaded with everything we've collected," Emily said. "It'll only take me a minute to go get it."

"I can go," Noah said.

"No. You stay here." She patted her holster to reassure him. "It's locked in the trunk, and I can't give you my keys without breaking protocol."

"You could zap it through the window after I get there," Noah said, looking down on the patrol car from the second-floor room.

Emily almost laughed. He was so endearing when he was trying to protect her in spite of her superior training and expertise. If she wasn't a cop, it would be tempting to let him act the hero. Only she *was* a cop, and she didn't need a civilian hero of any kind. She was her own defender, her own hero.

Calling, "Be right back," and waving as she passed through the doorway into the hall, she began to jog toward the stairwell. This nightmare would soon be over. She was positive of it. They already had two men in custody, and there was a fair chance Vangie would be able to ID more faces from the videos on the laptop, even if she failed to do so with her own recordings.

Emily had a good feeling about this visit. A very good feeling.

Mentally chastising herself because she kept picturing Noah instead of sticking to the task at hand, she had to keep pushing aside divergent thoughts.

Laptop. Upstairs. Vangie, she repeated in her mind.

Forget about that good-looking guy who keeps trying to take charge. Concentrate on the job at hand.

Leaving the building, she hurried to her car. Clicked the unlocking button on her key fob and saw…a flat tire.

A shiver skittered up Emily's spine like the icy tip-toeing of a spider on her skin. No threat was visible, but the evidence was clear.

With one hand on her gun, she spun in a circle, looking for signs. The lot was empty except for an older couple helping each other to their car.

She paused, intending to call her dispatcher, then realized she was far out of her district, so she grabbed up the computer, slammed the trunk and ran back toward the building.

NINETEEN

Noah had been watching Emily from the window in Vangie's room and saw the change in her demeanor. He didn't realize how easy he was to read until the patient asked him, "What's wrong?"

"Officer Zwalt just bent over to look at her car, then started back to us in a hurry. I'm trying to decide why."

"Maybe she just doesn't want to be gone too long."

"Maybe." Noah saw a dark-clad figure appear next to the police car and crouch down behind it. He eyed the hospital guard on duty. "I think somebody's messing with the car. Hold the fort. I'll be right back."

"You should wait here. I'll call hospital security."

"By the time you explain things, I can be there and back," Noah argued. The excuse to leave had involved the car. His real reason centered more on making sure Emily knew there was someone doing something to her patrol unit and getting there to confront them before they could do more damage.

A .357 automatic was tucked into a holster concealed at his waist, imparting a sense of power. He didn't have to brandish the gun to feel more self-assured. Just knowing he had it handy was enough.

Noah fully expected to encounter Emily on the stairs,

tell her what he'd seen and accompany her back down to the parking lot. When he didn't spot her, it was puzzling but not unnerving until he burst into the lobby and found it deserted.

Not slowing except to scan the visible areas of the ground floor, he pivoted and headed for the automatic doors that led outside. They slid open smoothly, quietly.

Noah squinted in the bright sun as he reached the entry portico, turned in a quick circle, then began to jog toward the parking lot. Instead of taking a direct path to the space reserved for official vehicles, he widened his approach by two lanes of cars in the hope he could sneak up on whoever had ducked behind Emily's unit.

Seeing no one, he approached cautiously. The police car had two flat tires that he could see, and judging by the way it appeared to be sitting level, he assumed the others were also deflated.

Noah pulled out his phone and thumbed Emily's cell number. The result was not a pleasant *Hello.* It was, "Where are you?" delivered with force.

"Downstairs. Where are you?"

"Where *you're* supposed to be." There was muffled conversation taking place in the background.

"Look out the window and you'll see me." He began to wave his free arm above his head. "Your car has flat tires."

"I saw. What I want to know is why you thought you had to interfere."

There were a lot of rebuttals Noah could have given. He refrained and settled on a simple, "I thought I could catch the vandal in the act."

"Did you?"

"No. Where did you hide while I was coming down? I didn't pass you on the stairs."

"I stopped to report the flat and ask security to call a tow truck."

"There's nobody by your car now. You want me to come back up, right?"

Her "Yes" was clipped, and she was clearly not happy.

"You'd have thanked me if I'd managed to nab the perp."

"Which you did not."

"Okay, okay. I was too slow. But I might have caught somebody."

Expecting her to continue to berate him, Noah ended the call and began to study the hospital's second-floor windows. Sun was reflecting off them as if they were sheets of gold foil, making it hard to identify what was going on inside.

All the windows but one looked blank. Third from the left showed rapid movement. Was that the room Emily was in? If so, he didn't like seeing such frantic-looking behavior. His phone jangled. It was her again. Instead of saying hello he asked, "Is that you jumping around up there?"

"Yes!" It was a hoarse shout. "Look out!"

Already tense, Noah had no doubt what she meant an instant later. Someone poked a hard object into the middle of his back and ordered, "Put down that phone."

Emily kept yelling into her cell phone until she realized Noah was no longer connected. She cupped her hands around her eyes and leaned against the window to try to see him more clearly. One thing was obvious. He wasn't alone anymore.

She'd already given the laptop to Vangie, so she addressed the guard. "Keep an eye on her and make sure she sticks to the files with the videos in them. I'll be right back."

Not waiting for a reply, she straight-armed the door, raced down the hallway and almost fell on the way downstairs because she was going so fast.

The automatic doors were just starting to open for her. She sidled through, went twenty feet into the portico, then slewed left. There was her patrol car.

Before she shouted, "Noah!" she knew. He was gone.

The person with the gun stayed behind Noah and directed his steps so he only managed a brief look at her. It was definitely a woman in the dark hoodie, but why accost *him*? Wasn't this stalker and probable killer after young women he'd befriended?

"Who are you?"

The barrel of the gun in her hand jabbed him in the back, causing added pain in the terrible bruise.

"Ow! Why did you shoot me?" he asked, wishing he didn't sound quite so angry.

"Stop lying. I never shot you," the woman grumbled.

"Yes, you did. And I can prove it." Noah crossed his hands in front of his body and started to loosen the bulletproof vest. He'd figured the armed woman would stop him, but she hesitated just long enough for him to lift his shirt and jacket and bare the injury to his back. He heard her gasp.

"Who did that to you? I'll settle with them."

"If it wasn't you, it was your partner."

"No way. Porter only did what I told him to."

One more question answered, Noah thought. Nevertheless, he'd have been a lot happier if he'd gotten that clarification in the police station, where there was no danger to himself or anyone else.

"Have you and Porter been friends long?" Noah asked, slipping his arms out of his jacket sleeves and letting it drop at his feet as he started to refasten the vest.

"Never mind us. Leave that," she ordered.

His intention had been to leave his jacket behind as a clue rather than the protective vest but the logo on it would be even better ID. He pulled his tee down, then donned the light jacket.

She waved the gun barrel to the right. "That way."

"Porter's been arrested, you know," Noah said.

"Yeah, I heard."

Noah's pulse was already fast. "Is that why you're here now? Did you come to finish the job he botched?"

"You're sure nosy."

"That's because I'm an attorney. We get used to asking questions."

Another look at the assailant shocked him. Her hoodie had fallen back, and her hair was bright red. That was a plus he hadn't counted on. Once Emily spotted them in the security cameras, there would be no mistaking who was who, and further investigation would lead her to the vest he was leaving behind to confirm it.

"I take it you and I knew each other in college?" he offered. "I'm sorry. I'm sure I'd remember that beautiful hair, but I don't."

Instead of the negative reaction he'd expected, the woman laughed. "Get moving before we have company, or I'll have to shoot your new girlfriend here and now."

"I thought a knife was your weapon of choice," Noah said.

"I use what I need to. Over there. The blue Kia. Get in."

Noah would have defied her if he hadn't seen a flash of movement near the disabled police car. *Emily?* Probably. He couldn't chance letting his captor take a shot at her. Not after all they'd been through. Still, once he got into the car he'd lose his size and weight advantage.

The arrival of a minibus full of senior citizens at the front door of the rehab facility sealed his decision. A shooting war under those circumstances was bound to injure innocent bystanders. He couldn't allow that. Not when he had an alternative.

"Who's driving, you or me?" he asked.

The woman flashed a momentary look of confusion, then said, "You are. I need to hold the gun."

Emily's view of the parking lot was cut off by a compact white bus. She dodged around it, straining on tiptoe to scan line after line of cars. The longer Noah was missing, the greater the risk of failing to recover him in one piece.

That concept reached into her core and tied knots in her already jangled nervous system. Of all the times for him to decide to stop being her shadow! What was he thinking? Time after time she'd assured him she could handle herself, and time after time he had refused to believe it, to trust her skills and discernment. If she wasn't so scared for him, she'd be furious.

Two armed security guards joined her. Emily whipped out her phone and thumbed through the picture file. "This is the man we need to locate," she said, flashing Noah's photo. "He was out here a few minutes ago. I believe he's been kidnapped."

The larger of the two guards was heavyset with extra chins bunched above his tight uniform collar. "What makes you think that?" he asked, obviously doubtful.

"Because I saw somebody sneak up behind him. He wouldn't have left of his own accord."

The guard shrugged at his partner. “Okay. What was he wearing?”

“A khaki jacket and jeans. Athletic shoes, I think, although I’m not positive if he had those on today.”

“Was he in custody?” the smaller, older guard asked.

“Custody? No. We were here to question a witness.”

“So, how did you two get separated?” the first man drawled, hooking his thumbs in his belt and tilting his head as if amused.

“Look,” Emily said firmly, “he was down here by my patrol car. I saw him from that window.” She pointed. “Somebody came up behind him while we were on the phone and cut us off. That’s all I know.”

“All right.” The big man pointed left and then right. “We’ll split up from here. You go down the center.”

Agreeing that the plan was as effective as any, Emily nodded and took off jogging. She didn’t want to go too fast and miss a clue, but she also didn’t want to delay. Something inside her kept insisting that passing seconds were critical.

Ambient noise created a hum around her while her pulse hammered in her ears. An engine revved to her left. Tires squealed. A small, dark blue sedan fishtailed at the exit and raced out into the street, causing passing drivers to brake and honk their horns.

Emily jumped onto a curb, straining to see better as the car passed a mere thirty feet away. The passenger’s hair was bright red and so thick and curly it partially obscured the driver.

Was that Noah behind the wheel, or was she seeing things because she so desperately wanted to?

A man shouted. Emily whipped around, losing sight of the departing vehicle. One of the guards was waving something black and yelling at her.

He’d found Noah’s bulletproof vest.

TWENTY

Emily was on the phone to her chief while she and the guards returned to the facility. "Yes, sir," she said. "We have every reason to believe Noah Holden has just been abducted. We're on our way to check the video from the parking lot cameras."

"All right. I'll coordinate with Memphis police and highway patrol. As soon as you have anything solid, we'll move."

"My car is out of commission," Emily admitted ruefully. "I'll need to hitch a ride with one of their units."

"Copy. Keep me posted."

The security office was little more than a cubbyhole. Three monitors focused on the parking lot. Some rapid movement was taking place as the guard on duty reversed the necessary recording, but it was impossible to get a clear enough picture to read the license plate of the car they suspected. The only clues they could make out were the blue color of the car and the red of someone's hair.

Crestfallen, Emily reported to her chief, then rode the elevator back to the second floor. She had been fighting tears ever since she'd first seen Noah being approached by the stranger, and the feeling of dread and loss kept growing.

One look at Vangie Mead's face, however, lifted her spirits. "I remembered something," the young blonde woman said.

"About Noah?"

"No. Somebody else." She was pointing at a freeze-frame on the computer screen. "That's Roz Carpenter Banfield. See how she looks mad at the world? She was always grumpy. That's what made me remember her."

Emily checked the timeline at the bottom of the video and made note of the number of that particular file, then phoned her chief. "We have a lead," she began. "Vangie, Ms. Mead, has identified that suspicious character seen watching Noah in one of the videos from his college days. It's Roz—probably short for Rosalind—Carpenter Banfield."

"All right. I'll see that a search for her is done immediately. Stay available. It shouldn't take long."

If Emily hadn't been with others, she would have let herself weep for joy. "Thank you, thank you."

"One more thing," Rowlings said. "The driver of the truck the officers pulled over for following you wasn't carrying ID, so it took awhile to get a name. It was Buddy Corrigan."

"Him? Why him?"

"That's unknown. We're looking for a connection to Nat Porter, and I'll add the Banfield woman."

"Okay, keep me posted."

"Will do."

Emily ended the call and turned to Vangie again. "Do you know anybody named Buddy Corrigan?"

"No. Was he in college with us, too?"

"I don't think so. He's lived in Paradise for as long

as I've known him." Emily switched subjects. "Did you ever see this Roz woman with bright red hair?"

When Vangie shook her head, Emily was disappointed. "Okay. I'm going to go downstairs to wait for reinforcements." She focused on the female guard. "Please keep an eye on our witness until you hear otherwise."

"Will do. Good luck," the guard said.

"I don't believe in luck," Emily vowed while her heart called out to God for wisdom, "but I do believe in taking action when it's called for. My cell number is on this card. Be sure to call me if Ms. Mead remembers anything else."

With that, she was out the door and headed for the lobby again. Each step served as a word of prayer, each breath confirmation that she was finally on the right track. She had to be. They had to be. Because Noah was gone, and it was her fault.

"Slow down before we get pulled over for reckless driving," Noah's captor ordered.

"I figured you'd want to get away fast."

"We don't have to speed. It's not far."

"Oh? Where are we going?"

"Somewhere quiet where we can talk, and no pretty blondes will distract you."

"Has that been a problem in the past?" The laugh she gave in reply was so cynical, Noah got chills. "I'm—I'm really bad with names. Sorry. What should I call you?"

"Darling would be nice."

"Sure, sure. I just thought a name would help me remember better. I know we were friends once."

"Not as close as I'd have liked, but I've fixed that now."

"That you have..."

"Roz. You can call me Roz or Linda."

"Ah, Rosalind," he said softly. "I do remember."

"Liar."

Noah did his best to appear calm. "Not at all. You used two last names, if I recall."

That brightened her countenance enough to assure him he'd guessed correctly, which was a relief of sorts. If he could remember that much, perhaps someone else would also identify this unbalanced woman. Sorting through his memory brought little additional information, so he chose to remain silent rather than make a mistake and upset her again.

"My gramma left me her place. I was positive I should keep it, and now I know why. It'll be ours, yours and mine. I know we can be happy there."

Noah held his peace. His idea of happiness had little in common with that of his captor, especially when it came to the people in his life. The more close brushes with death he experienced, the more he realized he'd closed himself off from life and the more he viewed Emily as an essential part of his future. If it wasn't too late.

His mouth was dry, his hands perspiring on the wheel. Every second he lived brought him closer to surviving this ordeal. There was no guarantee that his wishes for the future were in line with those of his Heavenly Father, although he hoped they were. Faith provided an avenue of prayer, but the answers that resulted couldn't be predicted. That was what faith was all about, he reminded himself: letting go and trusting God.

"Make a left at the next traffic light," Roz said.

A brief glance in the mirrors showed Noah that they were not being followed, and his spirits sagged. Had somebody found his discarded vest yet? Had the security system at the rehab hospital captured the license number of this car? Was there any way Emily could track him?

Suddenly, his heart leaped. Yes! His cell phone was still active. Even if no one figured out who had kidnapped him, the phone's signal should bring help. Eventually.

Continuing to feign calm, he reminded himself that a successful rescue depended on his staying alive despite a gun in the hands of someone so confused and obsessed. Wrestling it out of her grasp was an option. So was drawing his own hidden firearm. The problem with both of those ideas was the high probability that Roz would get off a shot before he was able to disarm her. Not only did he have himself to consider, he had to protect innocent passersby the way he had when she'd forced him into the car.

The best choice at this point was pretending to cooperate, Noah reasoned. Until everyone was in the clear, he needed to bide his time, what there was left of it, and wait for the right opportunity to act. The only problem with doing that was keeping control of his nerves and quelling the urge to go on the offensive. He knew he could probably escape if he was willing to hurt his captor, really hurt her. If all other options were gone, perhaps he would, yet memories from his past kept insisting he not cause others pain. If he'd learned anything by watching his abusive father, it had been to resist any tendencies to lose his temper and lash out.

"Turn left at the signal and keep going." Roz gestured with the barrel of the gun. "In about five miles, we'll come to a dirt road by a mailbox. That's where we're going."

Noah slowed and followed her directions. He'd been speeding in the hopes a traffic cop would pull them over. Now that that option was unlikely, he was in no hurry to reach their destination.

"That driveway over there," Roz finally said. "Pull through the gate."

Noah followed directions and stopped inside the yard, noting how isolated the property was. Her hand was resting on the door handle as if about to open it. If she got out to shut the gate, he might be able to throw the car into Reverse and back away before she could get off a shot. Was this his chance? Was it time?

He silently asked God for confirmation. Instead of the opportunity he'd asked for, Roz reached over and removed the key from the ignition.

Emily introduced herself to the two Memphis police officers who met her in the parking lot. "Zwalt," she said, repeating their names to reinforce her memory. "Robinson. Longacre. Thanks for your help."

Robinson was behind the wheel. "Where to?"

"I only have one lead so far. The name I reported. Rosalind Carpenter Banfield."

"One Banfield came up in our records," Longacre said. "What's the connection to your possible abduction?"

"Past history, we think," Emily said, eyeing the rear seat with trepidation as she got in. "Let's go."

As they pulled into traffic, Emily continued to fill them in. "Noah Holden was here in Memphis with me to help another witness identify people in an old video. He was armed. I don't understand why he didn't defend himself."

"Smart man," Robinson said. Longacre was nodding.

"Right. Starting a shoot-out in the middle of a city would have been idiotic. Your witness deserves a medal."

"I'd rather he thought of himself occasionally." Emily was leaning forward in the rear seat of the police car and speaking between them. "He's always too concerned about everybody else."

"Sounds like a great guy," the cop behind the wheel commented.

Emily struggled against the deep conviction that was washing over her. If she agreed that Noah was right, that meant she had to be wrong. This was more than a question of patience, wasn't it? It was about altruism, about putting others first. Becoming a trained officer of the law had been her answer to the pain of loss, but somewhere along the way to earning a badge, she'd lost the ability to see both sides of an argument. Was that what Noah had been trying to demonstrate?

Shaking herself free of such disturbing self-examination, Emily asked, "How much farther?"

"We're not sure we'll find the person of interest at this address," the driver's partner cautioned. "It was the only property in or near here that carried that same last name."

"I know, I know." And she did, but that didn't mean she was ready to relax or give up. Noah wouldn't have given up on her, would he? He'd proved that when he'd kept showing up in her life at the expense of his career. What Max would do when he got out of the hospital and realized how inefficiently Noah had been behaving on the job was unknown. She wouldn't blame the older man for firing his protégé on the spot. And then Noah would surely leave Paradise. Again. This time perhaps for good.

The minutes and miles passed rapidly as Emily pondered Noah's dilemma and the way he'd handled being the key to identifying a killer. Anger didn't seem to be part of his character, did it? That alone was impressive, although she couldn't help wondering if he was simply good at hiding his true emotions. Many attorneys were. They had to be to function in court to the advantage of their clients.

How Noah, or anybody else, managed to defend the guilty was beyond her, yet they did it. Getting a light sentence handed down to a dangerous criminal was, in her opinion, the same as excusing the crime, no matter who it hurt. How could she possibly be so fond of a man like that? she asked herself, realizing that her emotions were sabotaging the firm resolve she'd taken such pains to establish.

Slowing alerted Emily. Their mostly white ride with two narrow blue stripes bracketing a gold one would have been less noticeable if it hadn't sported a light bar across the top. Longacre picked up the mic. "Unit twelve on scene. Staging."

"Copy," their dispatcher replied. "Records show your suspect inherited that property. Advise need for backup."

"Understood," he said before looking back at Emily. "Wait here."

"What?"

"This is our call. You know the drill. You're out of your jurisdiction."

"I lost the witness, and I'm going after him." She pointed. "Unlock this door and let me out. Now."

The other officers didn't open the door and release her until they had checked with their superiors and received orders to do so. Once she was out of the car, she made up her mind that any future ride-along would take place only if she was seated in front. Yes, she would let the locals precede her into the yard. No, she wouldn't allow them to enter the house without her.

"I know the victim well, and you don't," she told them as she followed their stealthy approach via a neighbor's yard. "If it comes down to a split-second decision, I should be in the lead." For a few long seconds, she thought they might disagree, but they both nodded.

"We need to see what's visible through the windows first," Emily said. "If we spot more than one male, I'll ID my witness for you. The woman should have bright red hair."

"Nice of her to pick a color that stands out like that," Robinson quipped.

Emily wasn't amused. "If this person is who and what we suspect she is, there's nothing nice about her."

"Violent serial killers aren't usually women," Robinson observed.

"Yeah, well, we think this one is."

"No proof?"

"Not until we take her prints and DNA," Emily told them. "There were plenty of clues left behind. We just had nothing to compare them with."

"What does she want with your witness? Did he see her kill somebody?"

Emily shuddered. "No. He knew her in the past, and it's been suggested that she may be eliminating women she views as competition."

Longacre arched his eyebrows. "Pretty drastic. Holden must be a really good-looking guy."

"He's a lot more than that," Emily admitted. "His heart for people is extraordinary."

"Is that how he got himself into this mess?" Robinson asked as they closed in on the house.

That possibility had not occurred to Emily, but it was plausible. Noah had always been likable, even as a much younger man with a chip on his shoulder. The mature man he had become was more than attractive to her, so why shouldn't he appeal to other women, too?

The concept of other women in Noah's life hit her like a fist in the stomach, and for the first time since they'd started finding bodies in Paradise, she understood a little about what was driving Rosalind Banfield.

Approaching the side of the small farmhouse, Emily raised on tiptoe to peer in a window, then quickly ducked back. "It's him. He's in there. Looks like she's holding a gun."

"We should fall back and wait for backup," Longacre whispered hoarsely. His partner agreed.

"You can suit yourselves. I'm going in, with or without you."

"That may be the way you operate in a little town in Missouri, but that's not how it's done here."

She was adamant. "Fine. You can provide a distraction or not. It's up to you."

Watching the two make eye contact and reading reluctant agreement, Emily nodded. "Thanks."

"If this goes sideways, it's all on you," Robinson said flatly. "The next unit is only a few minutes out."

"A few minutes may be all we have," Emily said.

Concerned looks on their faces were proof they thought so too.

The interior of the closed-up house smelled musty, and Noah could see dust motes drifting in beams of sunlight peeking between the slats of the window blinds.

He waved a hand. "We should open some windows, air this place out."

"Shut up and sit down."

"Okay, okay. Take it easy. I was just trying to make it more comfortable in here. You said we're staying, right?"

"I decide," Roz insisted. "I'm in charge now, and I'll make the decisions for both of us."

"Sure. Fine." He perched on the edge of a hard chair next to the kitchen table, making sure to keep plenty of room around him for ease of maneuvering. As long as his captor held a gun ready to shoot, he didn't intend to rile her. Once she put it down, however, he'd be ready to take control of the situation. Noah didn't think it would be long. Tension sapped a person's strength, and maintaining absolute control had to be draining for his captor.

His heart would have gone out to her if she hadn't already proved how deadly she could be. Yes, he felt sorry for her, but no, he wasn't a fool. There was little doubt in his mind that Roz was capable of killing, even killing him, if her plans were thwarted and she saw no way out.

"Aren't you getting hungry?" Noah asked.

"No."

"I could check the fridge and see about fixing us something to eat. I'm a pretty good cook."

"Did you cook for all of them?" Roz asked, staring at him with evident malice. "You did, didn't you?"

"Who?"

"All those women."

"Not really."

"Don't lie to me. I saw you and that lady cop acting all cozy."

Noah had to clamp his jaw to keep from reacting the way he wanted to. Emily didn't resemble the women

Roz had eliminated, but they'd been wrong about that commonality, hadn't they? The serial killer hadn't been stalking blonde women. She'd been hunting innocent acquaintances from his past, women who probably had little memory of him after all this time. Therefore, if she began to suspect how much Emily meant to him, there would be nothing to stop her from carrying the vendetta into the present. Nothing except him.

"I was actually looking at old videos. That's where I saw you. Your plan was genius, you know."

"I was pretty smart, wasn't I? Took you from right under her ugly nose." Roz laughed cynically.

"You could have saved yourself the trouble," Noah said. "I like redheads, too. All you had to do was ask me, and I'd have met you anywhere you said."

"Sure, you would."

He stood slowly, cautiously, his hands spread, palms up. "I'm here, aren't I?"

"Yeah, well..." She reached up with her free hand, grabbed a fistful of red hair and gave her wig a yank. "What about now? I almost ruined my real hair trying to bleach it out so you'd notice me."

The wispy sparseness of her natural brown hair clearly showed damage. "I'm sorry you felt you needed to do that," Noah said.

"Yeah, well, if I'd known you'd take up with a lady cop with darker hair, I could have saved myself a lot of grief. I can't believe you broke your pattern with her."

Noah didn't think it would help to tell Roz that he'd never chosen his friends by their looks, so he kept it to himself. What was it that had attracted him to Emily so strongly? Her spirit? Her quick mind? Her wit? Or had there been an intrinsic connection all along? He had no clue, nor did it matter. Emily was a unique individual who posed a challenge to his preconceived notions beyond anything he'd experienced before. Not only did she disparage his career choice, she ran around with a chip on her shoulder the size of a bus. Surely there were more agreeable women to choose from than Emily Zwalt.

Only he didn't want anyone else, did he? Noah's mind finally agreed with what his heart had been insisting for some time. He cared for Emily so deeply that he already thought of her as his future. Therefore, he better understood how hard the loss of her fiancé had hit her and why it had warped her attitude toward courts and attorneys.

He was about to try more flattery in the hope of winning the killer's confidence when they were both startled by a knock on the front door. Noah was immediately thankful the loud noise hadn't caused Roz to squeeze the trigger, because she'd been waving the gun around carelessly, and there was no telling where her bullets might have gone.

"Stay behind me while I go see who's here," she ordered. "And keep your mouth shut."

"No problem." Hanging back as far as he dared, he accompanied her through the dusty living room and stood aside while she unlocked the front door and opened it a crack.

Outside on the porch, a smiling police officer greeted her. "Sorry to bother you, ma'am. We're canvassing the neighborhood for the sheriff's youth program. Would you care to make a donation?"

"No. I'm busy."

The officer touched the bill of his cap and nodded politely, backing away. "Sorry to bother you. Thanks for your time."

Noah was just about to sigh with relief when he

caught a flash of movement out of the corner of his eye and made an instant connection.

No! His breath fled. His fists clenched. He braced himself.

Emily. Emily was in the house.

TWENTY-ONE

Heart about to pound out of her chest, Emily faded into the shadows and prayed the armed killer wouldn't get nervous and decide to shoot Noah before she was able to disarm her. Not knowing the layout of the old house was a definite disadvantage. By entering through the unlocked rear door, she had taken a calculated risk. The same was true of allowing Noah to get a glimpse of her.

Footsteps echoed as kidnapper and victim went back into the kitchen. Emily followed as best she could without showing herself again. Noah now knew she was there with him. Hopefully, that knowledge would keep him from doing something stupid and getting himself killed.

The moment that thought entered her mind, she began to tremble. This was the first instance in two years as a cop that armed conflict had affected her this way. Oh, she'd had to decompress from previous incidents involving deadly force, sure, but those encounters had never given her the shakes or made her stomach roil this way.

Conversation was coming from the kitchen, so she crept closer to eavesdrop.

"Look out the window and tell me if the cops are gone," Roz was telling Noah.

"I'm sure they are," he said. "You handled yourself quite well."

The voice grew shrill. "Do as I say. Look."

"Okay, okay."

Emily could picture his calm demeanor, the way he always raised his hands slightly as if indicating surrender. That practiced facade would be necessary now, more than ever.

Making the assumption that this killer was not rational, Emily stayed out of sight. What the others did from here on would determine her next moves.

"I don't see any police car," Noah told Roz.

"I don't believe you."

"Then look for yourself."

To do so, Roz would have to face one of the kitchen windows, meaning she'd temporarily turn away from the hall. Emily took a chance and peered around the corner.

Noah saw her immediately, warning her off with a frown and slight shake of his head.

In those few seconds Emily did a threat assessment. Whether or not Noah had been disarmed, Roz was holding him at gunpoint, and he'd left his protective vest behind. That made a surprise attack too risky. It also meant that, in her efforts to trap the killer, she had also trapped herself and Noah.

They were stuck in the house together, and Emily's only advantage at the moment was that Noah knew she was there.

Roz started to turn.

Emily ducked back out of sight. A split second separated their actions. It was too long.

A bullet smacked into the wall above Emily's head.

She ducked, swung around the corner and slipped her finger inside the trigger guard, ready to shoot back.

Noah had pulled his own weapon and was aiming it at Roz.

There they stood, all three of them, all armed, all ready to fire. Nobody moved.

Noah shouted. “Freeze!”

“Police!” Emily yelled at the same time.

Roz didn’t seem fazed by the firepower trained on her, and that frightened Noah more than anything.

He stood his ground. So did Emily. If he shot at Roz, there was a very good chance her gun would go off too, and it was aimed right at the love of his life. Even if Em got off a shot of her own and wounded Roz, it probably wouldn’t be enough to stop the chain reaction.

Somebody had to break the standoff, he reasoned, and it would have to be him.

He cleared his throat then forced a smile and lowered his gun. “Settle down, ladies. I’ve made my choice. There’s no reason to get excited.”

Roz never wavered. Neither did Emily, so he moved slowly to stand between the women with his attention on the killer. “It’s going to be okay. I’ll see that the police leave.”

“I don’t believe you.”

Instead of laying the weapon aside, he cautiously slid it into his pocket, relieved when Roz raised no objection. The use of soft words and smooth motions seemed to be helping, so he continued by lifting his hands slightly. “Suppose I can get this officer to put her gun away and leave the house. Will that do?”

“Do for what?” Roz countered. “Do you think I’m a fool? I’ve seen the way you look at her.”

"We used to be friends when we were kids, that's all," he alibied.

"Yeah, right."

Behind him, Noah heard Emily breathing hoarsely, as if she might be about to act, although what she thought she could do under these circumstances was a mystery.

Chancing a step he moved closer to the armed woman, wondering if she could fire faster than he could knock the gun aside. It was likely she could, especially if she anticipated his move.

This was a masters chess competition with real people as critical game pieces and the timer ticking off the seconds. Not moving was harder than it would be to act, yet he knew better than to force things.

The sound of multiple sirens as more law enforcement arrived was building. Noah took a deep breath before he offered, "Look, Roz. It doesn't sound good out there. Let me intervene for you so nobody else gets hurt. I can talk to them. Calm everybody down. What do you say?"

"Ha! You think I'm a fool? I know you're lying."

"Actually, I'm not," Noah promised. "I can go out and explain to them that you want to surrender."

"Who says I do?"

"You're an intelligent woman. Surely you see how this has to end."

"Not unless I lay down this gun."

Noah was acutely aware that his body was the only thing standing between Roz's bullets and Emily. Even though Em was wearing a vest, it might not save her at this distance, and that was assuming the shot was aimed at her upper torso and nowhere else. It was simply too much of a chance to take. He had to stand his ground.

Roz motioned with the pistol barrel. "Move out of the way and let me end this."

"I'm sorry. I can't do that."

"Then I'll shoot you first."

Hair on the nape of his neck prickled. Trembling inside, he did his best to appear confident. "I thought you liked me. Didn't all those girls have to die because they came between us?"

"So what? If I can't have you, nobody can."

Instinct told Noah that drawing Roz into conversation was helping to split her focus, so he continued as if arguing a case in court. "Are you saying they'd still be alive if I hadn't paid attention to them? That hardly seems the most accurate way to choose."

"Accurate enough. I brought them to you, didn't I? Delivered your girlfriends right to your door?"

"Is that how they ended up in Paradise? Why didn't you just leave them where they were?"

"Because you wouldn't have known they were gone. You had to know you were free to choose me."

"That was a mistake, you know. If you hadn't crossed state lines the FBI wouldn't have posted your crimes to their Violent Criminal Apprehension Program."

Roz screeched at him. "I'm not a criminal! I keep trying to tell you that but you're not listening. Nobody listens to me."

"What about the guys who were helping you? They must have believed you."

"I don't know what you're talking about."

"Really? How about Buddy Corrigan? He's the one who lured me to the park after you eliminated my client."

"I don't know any Buddy whatever-his-name-is. And I didn't tell you to come to any park."

"What about the client you put in the hospital? Laura Bright?"

Roz seemed surprised and slightly subdued. "Yeah, well, I am kind of sorry about her. Any woman who puts up with a man like her husband deserves a break. I just had to finish what I'd started, you know?" She snorted derisively. "I should have rammed that cleaning cart into your cop friend much harder."

"Well, you did scare her good." Pausing, Noah waited until Roz finished chuckling. "I wish you hadn't cut me, though. My arm still hurts."

"That wasn't me," she countered. "That was Porter. I told him to stay away from you."

"So, let me get this straight," Noah drawled, trying to sound convincingly nonchalant. "You and your helper were not responsible for my client dying in the Paradise park?"

"Are you dense? I already told you that."

Noah slowly lifted one arm and held out his open hand. "Give me the gun, *darling*." A slight softening around her eyes encouraged him. "Please?"

For a few moments he actually had hope. Then, as if the hate inside her was rising, her brow furrowed, and she started to shake her head.

It was now or never, he told himself. As long as Emily held her fire, this might actually work. What choice did he have? All he could hope at this point was that Emily would understand and forgive him if he got himself killed trying to save her.

Standing directly behind Noah, Emily kept her finger off the trigger while remaining primed for action. What in the world had possessed him to put himself in this kind of jeopardy? Apprehending criminals was her job, not his, and by interfering, he'd figuratively tied her hands.

She caught a tiny twitch of a shoulder muscle as he spoke to his kidnapper. The man was an unbelievably good actor in the face of possible death. Of course he was scared. So was she. But they had to keep calm and behave rationally despite the actions of such an unbalanced foe.

There it was again. Emily's finger slipped inside the trigger guard just enough to provide access in a split second.

The scene in front of her seemed to drop into slow motion. Noah's already extended arm swung across his body, the flat of his hand hitting the side of the assailant's gun and smacking it to one side.

Emily threw herself in the opposite direction, rolled and came up with her weapon aimed at Roz.

Both fired.

Roz's bullet went wild, shattering a decorative plate on the kitchen wall.

Emily had better aim. Her shot caught the killer in the shoulder and spun her around.

Noah wrapped Roz in a tight hold and kept her arms pinned at her sides while she screamed and bled from the superficial wound.

Back and front doors shattered simultaneously.

The kitchen filled with police officers from two states and several dark-suited FBI agents. Law enforcement separated the victims from the criminals with Emily's help, and an ambulance was called to treat the injured woman.

Noah plunked himself down into one kitchen chair, and Emily took a second one. She relinquished her duty weapon as standard procedure and watched paramedics make sure Noah wasn't the one who'd been bleeding.

The longer she sat there and decompressed, the more deflated she felt. This degree of weariness wasn't normal for her, but then, neither was being part of an armed standoff with a confessed murderer.

Thankfulness didn't begin to cover her emotions. Neither did relief. Love was mixed in there somewhere, too, she admitted, although considering the presence of so many other officers, she chose to keep that to herself.

One thing was certain. Noah had saved her when she'd been out of options, and his glib tongue was an integral part of his arsenal. Hostage negotiators were trained to do the same, but for Noah, the skill seemed to come naturally. No wonder he'd been such a success as a defense attorney. And no wonder Max valued him so highly.

Thinking of Max Maxwell reminded Emily of his relationship with Olivia Brooks, a closeness that might never have come to light without the stroke that had sidelined him. That was a great example of God bringing good out of what at first seemed like tragedy.

So it was here, too, Emily concluded. The terrible crimes had not only been solved, but the solution had led her to fully appreciate Noah Holden's skills and courage.

Catching his eye across the kitchen table, she smiled slightly. "It's over. Finally."

Because she'd expected agreement, she was put off when he shook his head and said, "No. Not quite."

"You *believed* her?" Emily asked. "The murder in the park fit the pattern of the other killings perfectly."

"I don't care," Noah said flatly. "I don't think she'd admit to every other murder and attack except one."

"You think Buddy did it?"

"Not necessarily."

"Then who?"

"Maybe Sam Fielding, the ex Charity had requested the restraining order against? Maybe someone entirely different. I just don't think we can wrap this all up in a pretty bow and pin everything on Roz."

Emily was flabbergasted. "You're *defending* her."

"I guess I am." Noah shrugged.

"Is that why you kept her talking? I thought it was because you were being smart, not devious."

"The truth is the truth, Emily," Noah said.

She would have been a lot happier if he hadn't sounded quite so positive.

TWENTY-TWO

The idea that Charity Roskov had been attacked by someone other than Rosalind Banfield was etched in Noah's mind. What he wanted to do was discuss the concept calmly with Emily ASAP and see if they couldn't work out the answer to the puzzle together.

A couple of aspects bothered him, especially when he felt the ache of the injury to his back. Roz had admitted that her cohort had used the knife on his arm but had vehemently denied shooting at him at all, let alone with a rifle. That fact was more than a bit unnerving, especially given Emily's choice to lump all the attacks together.

If he went over her head and spoke to her chief, she'd be furious with him. If he didn't, and there was a second killer, he might not live to continue their argument. Of course there was always the FBI, he reasoned, figuring he'd be hard-pressed to get any of those agents to listen to his concerns. They were focused on one thing—the series of similar killings. Lesser incidents that might or might not be connected would be sorted out later. The only problem with that, in Noah's mind, was the immediacy of the personal threat, assuming he was right about being targeted at least twice.

He flexed his shoulder blades and felt twinges of lingering pain. In his opinion, the shot into the police car had been too accurate to be random. Someone had been aiming. The only real question at this point was whether or not the shooter had known he was the man in the passenger seat.

His first stop the following day was his office. As soon as he'd caught up a little there and visited an incarcerated felon, he headed for the PPD. Chief Rowlings shook his hand and invited him into the privacy of his office.

Noah got right down to business. "I have a problem."

"I hope it doesn't have anything to do with your college dating days," Rowlings joked, grinning.

Noah remained stoic. "No. It's something else."

"Go ahead. I'm listening."

"Charity Roskov. I'm assuming you've been briefed on the possibility she was murdered by someone other than the serial killer in custody."

"It was mentioned."

"What about the indictment? Do you expect to include her case?"

"The FBI thinks we should."

"Fingerprints? DNA? Is there anything to refute that conclusion?"

"I can't disclose those details. You know that."

Noah sighed. "Suppose I was Rosalind Carpenter Banfield's attorney of record."

"That's a conflict of interest."

"Not until a judge rules it is." He withdrew a folded piece of paper from his coat pocket and showed it to the chief. "She signed a contract in her cell this morning."

Shaking his head, Rowlings began to pace. "How

can you be serious about offering an unbiased defense? Nobody is that forgiving."

"I didn't say I forgave her, although I think I have. She's ill. That's going to be my argument if I'm still representing her when this goes to trial."

"And you really don't think she tried to shoot you? After what happened in that kitchen?"

"That was a reflex. I'd anticipated it." He approached the older man to speak more quietly. "I don't think my client, or her associate, Nat Porter, would have purposely targeted me, that's all. She should be tried for the crimes she committed, not for everything on your books." He'd been tempted to add, *Just because it's easy*, but refrained. Accusations weren't wise, nor were they necessarily accurate in this case, although it did seem as if Emily Zwalt was more than willing to place all the blame on one person.

"All right," the chief said. "The FBI crime lab did manage to isolate a couple samples of male DNA from the body in the park. One matches yours."

"And the other?" Noah was holding his breath.

"We have nobody to pair it with."

"What about Fielding, the ex she wanted the restraining order against?"

"His is not on file."

"Have you tried to get a court order for a sample?"

"Yes, as a matter of fact, we did that early on. He seems to have disappeared."

Noah's brain was spinning. "So, you haven't eliminated him."

"Not completely. As her former boyfriend, it's possible he left traces before the night of the actual crime, you know."

"Yeah, sure." Heading for the door, Noah pocketed

the signed agreement. "You may want to inform Officer Zwalt. She seems pretty sure he wasn't involved."

"That she does. Can you tell me why?"

Nodding, Noah was positive he got the true picture. It was disturbing, yet understandable. "Yes," he said. "She may not realize or admit it, even to herself, but she's delighted to blame my new client for any and everything. I'm not going to enjoy proving her wrong, but it has to be done."

"To make a point?"

"Not about my client, no," Noah said. "About the dangers of believing we're always right just because we represent the law. Sometimes the best of our abilities fall frighteningly short. Failing to admit mistakes and exercise forgiveness hurts everybody, no matter how pure our motives may be."

Reliving the scene of Noah disarming the killer and recalling the echo of the shots inside the small house played in Emily's mind like an endless loop of video. She had far too little work to do thanks to having to wait for an official adjudication on the necessity for discharging her firearm, and that gave her plenty of thinking time.

Following procedures wasn't excuse enough. She had to justify her actions via the only witness present other than the criminal. Therefore, Noah Holden had been summoned to the station to testify before an investigating committee. It was personally disappointing to see how standoffish he was acting when he arrived.

"I'd like to speak with Officer Zwalt, if I may," she heard Noah say. Naturally the request was going to be denied, probably even after he'd been deposed. As the only witness, it was going to be up to him to exonerate her. Or not. Although she couldn't imagine a scenario in which he blamed her.

She caught his attention from across the office and didn't smile. This infraction could be serious enough to cost her to lose her career if it wasn't properly handled. This was the first time she'd been officially involved in a situation where deadly force was called for, and she had been second-guessing her decision to shoot ever since.

Was that the way Jake had felt back then? Was that why he'd held his fire when he could have fought back? The supposition was so plausible it hurt to consider. She got it now. All of it, from the choice to hold fire all the way up to the decision to pull the trigger. Less than a heartbeat of time might stand between seeing a need and acting upon it or choosing to stand down instead. This was not something that could be rationally considered ahead of time. To try to do so was self-defeating because the wrong choice at the wrong time could get a cop killed. In the case of her former fiancé, it had.

Emily was still at her desk half an hour later when she heard Noah's voice again. He was bidding the investigators goodbye. Was she in the clear now? One look at his expression assured her she was, and she rose to meet him. "Thanks."

"I just told the truth."

"That's all I ask."

"Good, because I have something else we need to discuss."

Her heart leaped, and her pulse sped. Was he finally going to admit what the killer had sensed all along? Was he going to confess tender feelings for her? She smiled. "Sure. Shall we go someplace private?"

To her surprise and disappointment, he said, "No. Here is fine."

"Okay..."

"I want to question Buddy Corrigan, and I want you to come with me."

"Why? They let him go because they couldn't prove he was following us."

"I plan to ask him about that second man in the park. The one who hit you over the head."

"What makes you think Buddy was involved at all? The killer could have been the Banfield woman and her accomplice, that Porter guy."

"Then why did Buddy phone me?"

"Last I heard, you doubted it was him at all."

"Suppose I was wrong?"

"Hah! You? Wrong? Never." Personal disappointment had crept in and was wreaking havoc with her responses. She'd been ready to tell Noah how she was growing to accept his career and confess how much she'd started to care for him, maybe even love him, yet all he wanted to do was rehash a solved crime.

As Emily analyzed his expression, it struck her that she might have pushed him a little too far. Being decisive was one thing. Acting disrespectful was another.

"Okay, I'm sorry," she said. "I take it you know where to find Buddy."

"If he's true to form, he'll be having breakfast in the Paradise Café. That's where I planned to start."

She glanced toward the chief's office, then made up her mind. "Since I'm still officially on desk duty, there's no reason why I can't take a few minutes to go with you."

It would have pleased Emily more to be in full uniform with her duty belt and gun, but since the serial killer and her henchman were safely locked away, it wasn't a big concern. After all, this was Paradise. Nothing much ever happened here, right?

She fell into step with Noah. "I wish they'd released my duty weapon. I feel vulnerable without it."

"Not to worry. I'm carrying."

"Could have fooled me." Emily preceded him through the door while he held it for her.

"That's why they call it concealed," Noah quipped.

The change of roles bothered her enough to say so. "I'd still feel better if I was carrying all my gear."

Noah chuckled quietly as they crossed the street bordering the town square and approached the café. "After the trick shooting I saw you do yesterday, I almost agree."

Intent on his mission, Noah entered the café first. Buddy was in the same booth at the rear, as he'd predicted. What he hadn't counted on was there being a second man with him. Viewed from the back, the enormous stranger in a grungy denim jacket and frayed baseball cap was unidentifiable.

Noah paused next to the table. "Good morning."

Corrigan jumped as if he'd just been shocked by a Taser. His companion froze, then slowly slid out of the booth and stood, towering over Noah's ample six-foot height. Menace was clear in the man's dark eyes, and his fists were clenched.

"Sam Fielding. Well, well." Noah gave Emily a subtle nudge to tuck her behind him, then offered to shake hands. The offer was ignored.

"That's right," Sam said, leering. "You probably saw pictures of me, didn't you? Charity Roskov was my woman."

"My condolences, Mr. Fielding," Noah said. "I didn't know you and Buddy were friends."

"Half brothers," the man explained. "Same mama." He chuckled. "My daddy was a mite bigger than his."

"That explains why I didn't put it all together," Noah said, wondering what was going to happen next.

Fielding tucked a meaty hand in his jacket pocket and gestured. "Let's go."

"I have no quarrel with you," Noah said, maintaining a calm facade. "I came to talk to Buddy. I can catch him later."

"You can talk to both of us now," Fielding said. His voice was low, yet the confrontation was catching the attention of diners nearby. Some had already slipped out of their seats and headed for the door, urging others to follow by pointing and whispering. Noah was happy to see people clearing out. He just wished he and Emily were among them.

Hands slowly rising to waist level, Noah spread his palms wide. Suddenly, there was a tiny brush against his back, a centered pressure that eased, a barely perceptible lightness, and he knew exactly what was happening. *"No."*

The other man obviously assumed Noah was talking to him and answered accordingly. "I say, yes."

"No, that's *crazy*."

"Who you callin' names, Mr. Lawyer? Huh?" Fielding gestured with the hand that was still in his pocket. "Go on. Through the kitchen and out the back where we won't be disturbed."

Noah didn't move. He didn't dare because he wasn't sure what Emily had done with the handgun she'd slipped out of his hidden holster. The .357 wasn't enormous as guns went, but it wasn't small, either. There was no way she could safely hide it on her person, and if Fielding or his half brother caught sight of it, game over.

Actually, the more Noah considered the mess they were in, the less chance he saw of escaping unharmed. Allowing himself to be marched out the back door into the alley where he could be disposed of in private didn't sound like a good idea. Neither did standing there trying to hide Emily's actions. Their choices were bad and worse.

"I need to say something first," Noah ventured. Instead of waiting for permission, he forged ahead. "The last few weeks have been the worst of my entire life." He cleared his throat and turned his head slightly. "They've also been some of the best…because of you."

With his arms still held slightly away from his body, Noah turned partway, then continued further when Fielding didn't stop him. Facing Emily, he shook his head and sighed. "I'm sorry we never had a chance to talk about what was happening between us. I think we might have made a go of it."

She nodded, misty-eyed. "I know."

"I had to tell you how I feel. Before…" His own vision began to blur as the seriousness of their situation settled in his heart. "None of this is your fault. I didn't take the time to look into the background of my client's stalker when I should have, and now here we are."

"I should have taken your good advice more seriously," Emily countered. "It's as much my fault as yours."

"Actually, it's Fielding's fault if you get right down to it." Noah glanced over his shoulder when he heard the snick of a knife opening. Buddy was cringing in the booth while his big brother held a lethal-looking weapon at the ready, its blade glistening in the overhead lighting.

Emily now had the superior weapon, Noah knew, but how was he going to tell her without setting off this killer? Any quick movements were bound to cause Fielding to attack, and a sharp blade in the hands of an expert could do plenty of damage before the off-duty cop could get off a safe shot, particularly with an unfamiliar weapon.

Right now, Buddy was directly in the line of fire, and even if she only meant to wound and disarm the man with the knife, her bullet could easily pass through him and hit his brother. Therefore, she was unlikely to fire.

The task Noah set for himself was to maneuver everyone around without letting the other men figure it out, then hope and pray that Emily would size up the situation in time to stop Fielding from lunging and ending one or both of their lives.

With one arm around her shoulders he urged her closer. Emily resisted. She pushed back against his chest, flicked off the gun's safety with her thumb and ducked around him, coming up in a shooter's stance, hands together in front of her.

Buddy screamed like a girl.

Noah shouted.

Emily held her fire long enough to say, "Drop it."

When Fielding raised the knife in his fist and started to bring it down in an arc, right at Noah, she did the only thing she could. She shot him in the hand.

Three lingering bystanders lunged at Fielding, took him to the floor and held him down while uniformed police swarmed in through the front door and rushed out of the kitchen to take over.

Noah was through waiting, through biding his time,

done being cautious. He relieved Emily of the gun, handed it to one of the cops, swept her up in his arms and kissed her until they were both breathless.

She was smiling when he let go long enough to look into her eyes and say, "Not sorry."

"Me neither," she replied. "I wouldn't want to go through any of this again, but since it's over, I guess it's okay to be thankful it brought out the best in you."

"In both of us," Noah said, having trouble waiting to hear her agree.

"Yes," Emily said, looking up at him lovingly. "Both of us."

That was all Noah needed to hear. "Do you think you could ever get used to being the wife of an attorney?"

She smiled. "I don't know. How do you feel about being the husband of a cop?"

"Honestly, it terrifies me, but we can make it work. I know we can," Noah said. "I'd never ask you to quit your job."

Sighing, Emily slipped her arms around him and nestled in his embrace. "You won't have to. I plan to use the time Internal Affairs takes investigating me to rethink my career. I really don't enjoy shooting people."

He pulled her closer and kissed her hair. "Whatever you decide to do, please say you'll do it with me in your life."

Emily laughed lightly. "Absolutely. I've been thinking of becoming a jungle safari guide and taking boatloads of tourists down the Amazon. How does that sound?"

"Like something you might actually try," he countered. "Don't worry, I'll negotiate your contracts to film it all, and we can sell it as a TV documentary."

"Let's start with planning something simpler, something local, like maybe getting married," Emily suggested with a sweet smile.

"Honey," Noah drawled, "I'm pretty sure that being married to you is going to be anything but simple. And I wouldn't have it any other way."

* * * * *

Dear Reader,

The jobs of enforcing the law and seeking justice can be extremely difficult, especially in a small town or close-knit neighborhood where so many people know each other. The same goes for paramedics and firefighters, doctors and nurses, emergency responders and more. These dedicated people have chosen to sacrifice their time, talents and sometimes even their lives to help others, and often it's so hard to do that it drops them to their knees.

Whether they realize it or not, they are following in the steps of Jesus by loving their neighbors as they love themselves. Are they perfect? Are any of us? Not a chance, but they, like most of us, are doing the best they can with the training they've had and the gifts they've been given. Until we're in the same position, we can't know how hard it is to do the right thing and accept the outcome regardless, but they know all too well.

Although our personal trials may look insurmountable, help is available. God knows your troubles. Jesus will take your hand and lift you up. Just reach out. Ask Him. Trust Him.

I can be reached easily by email, Val@ValerieHansen.com, or through my website, www.ValerieHansen.com.

Be Blessed,
Valerie Hansen

LOVE INSPIRED SUSPENSE
INSPIRATIONAL ROMANCE

The body count is mounting—
and a target is on their backs

Stumbling upon a murder is the biggest shock of Noah Holden's life—until he learns he knew the victim. When more women from his past are killed, Noah needs Officer Emily Zwalt's help to remove his name from the top of the list of prime suspects. But when the serial killer acquires a new target, they must work together before Emily becomes the next victim.

AN EMERGENCY RESPONDERS THRILLER